EXODUS/UK

EXODUS/UK
RICHARD ROHMER

A TOTEM BOOK
TORONTO

First published, 1975, by
McClelland and Stewart Limited,
Toronto, Canada

This edition published 1976
by TOTEM BOOKS
a division of
Collins Publishers
100 Lesmill Road, Don Mills, Ontario

© 1975 Richard Rohmer
All rights reserved

ISBN 0 00 222083 0

Printed in Canada by
Universal Printers Ltd. Winnipeg

Books by Richard Rohmer

The Green North Mid-Canada (1970)
The Arctic Imperative (1973)
Ultimatum (1973)
Exxoneration (1974)

To all the Olivias
who have been and are
in my life

Olivia Mark
Carrie Olivia Whiteside
Mary Olivia Whiteside Rohmer
Catherine Olivia Rohmer

The continent of North America, if properly cultivated, will prove an inexhaustible fund of wealth and strength to Great Britain; and perhaps it may become the last asylum of British liberty, when the nation is enslaved by domestic despotism or foreign dominion; when her substance is wasted, her spirit broke, and the laws and constitution of England are no more: Then those colonies, sent off by our fathers, may receive and entertain their sons as hapless exiles and ruined refugees.

The London Chronicle for 1758, Feb. 2-4

Exodus/U.K.

Prime Minister of Great Britain	JEREMY SANDS
Chancellor of the Exchequer	MICHAEL HOBSON
Foreign Secretary (U.K.)	PETER STANTON
President of the United States	DANIEL SHEPPARD
Governor of the Bank of England	SIR RICHARD PILLING
Secretary of State for Scotland	ANGUS STEWART
Minister of Health and Social Security	MARGARET WRIGHT
Prime Minister of Canada	JOSEPH ROUSSEL
Minister of Environment (U.K.)	AGNES POTTER
Home Secretary (U.K.)	SIR BENJAMIN WICKS
Secretary of State for Trade and Industry (U.K.)	MALCOLM ROSS
Defence Secretary (U.K.)	LORD JOHN CUTTING
Leader of the Opposition (U.K.)	THOMAS SHORT
Private Secretary to Sands	ROGER PRENTICE
VC-10 Captain	S/L BASIL ROBINS
VC-10 First Officer	F/L CRANSTON
VC-10 Engineer	F/O JASON RUPERT
Principal Secretary to Roussel	PIERRE PRATTE
Minister of Finance (Can.)	ANDRÉ VACHON
Wife of the Prime Minister (Can.)	MANON ROUSSEL
Premier of British Columbia	OSCAR BULLIT
Secretary of Labor (U.S.)	LINCOLN HAMILTON
Secretary of the Treasury (U.S.)	HERMAN SCHWARTZ
Minister for External Affairs (Can.)	YVES PARENT
Secretary of the Cabinet (U.K.)	SIR PETER FLOOD

Monday, July 5

The Prime Minister couldn't believe what he was hearing.

The Chancellor of the Exchequer was adamant. "There is absolutely no doubt about my information," he said. "My source is totally reliable. The Arabs have decided to cut off all investments in the U.K. and to withdraw all of their money deposited in our banking system – as of today."

"But that's impossible," the Prime Minister replied. "It'll mean disaster. Absolute disaster."

The two men stood motionless in the entrance hall of 10 Downing Street. The Chancellor of the Exchequer, Michael Hobson, a dripping umbrella still in his hand, thought back to the early call that brought him the shocking news. Finally, Prime Minister Jeremy Sands, still dressed in pyjamas and dressing gown, turned away and shuffled slowly across the checkered floor to the inner hall, then past the Green Room to the library which he used as an office. He walked around the long Cabinet table to the huge ancient leather chair at the centre of the table in front of the cold fireplace. The Prime Minister slumped into it, his mind racing with the ramifications of this dreadful news. Hobson, having deposited his wet umbrella in the entrance hall rack, followed the Prime Minister into the library, where he sat in the armchair opposite Sands. Leaning forward, hands clenched, elbows on his knees, the Chancellor showed no outward sign of his inner agitation.

"Well Michael, what's this all about?"

Hobson began. "A little less than an hour ago, I received a call from Enright, the managing director of Heap & Sons Limited, the principal London financial agents for the Saudis. Enright and I were classmates at the London School of Economics, close friends and all that sort of thing."

The Prime Minister nodded knowingly.

"He told me he had just received telephone instructions from the Saudi Finance Minister – from Riyadh – directing him to cancel forthwith all instructions for further Saudi investments in the U.K., to withdraw all funds on deposit with any British banks, and to serve notice that all monies on short-term deposit will be called on their due dates and transferred out of the country in accordance with instructions that will be received later in the day."

"But why?"

"Evidently there was an emergency summit conference of Arab oil-producing countries yesterday, at the call of the Saudi King. He was informed by his intelligence people that contrary to his explicit instructions to the government of the United Kingdom, we had secretly shipped one hundred complete Rapier ground-to-air missile systems to the Israelis. I told Enright that, so far as I knew, no such shipment had taken place. Nothing's ever come before Cabinet . . ."

The Prime Minister's bushy eyebrows arched slightly. He ran his hand through his tousled mane of white hair and shifted uncomfortably. Then he began, his voice low and gravelly: "Michael, my dear fellow, the matter of Rapiers for Israel did not get to the Cabinet. I authorized the sale myself and gave private instructions to the appropriate ministers. God knows we need all the export dollars we can get, and the

14

sale means many millions, which the Israelis have agreed to pay in American dollars. You know the figures better than I, Michael. They're your figures. We're running a trade deficit every month – visible current account – of almost 550 million pounds, over a billion dollars. The only thing that's been keeping us alive, afloat if you will, is the money the Arabs have been investing here in real estate, in corporations, and particularly in short-term deposits with our banks. It comes to just about a billion dollars a month, and it's been just enough to keep our economy from collapsing totally."

"But, Jeremy," the alarmed Chancellor exclaimed, "the Arabs told you that under no circumstances was Britain to ship arms to Israel. It was no more than two months ago that the Saudi ambassador delivered a note saying that they and the other Arab oil-producing states would find any further shipment of arms to Israel unacceptable. You knew that any breach, any shipment to Israel, would make the Arabs furious!"

The Prime Minister nodded. "You're quite right, Michael. But on the other hand, we've been on good terms with the Arabs for many decades. I thought that when they found out they would raise absolute hell with us – even threaten reprisals if it happened again – but I didn't think they would go this far. They've got so much invested here on long term. If they pull out on us now, they'll lose billions because we simply won't be able to pay." He paused. "Too bad King Faisal was assassinated. He wouldn't have gone this far."

Hobson jumped to his feet. "Surely you ought to have been able to foresee what the Arabs would do if they found out. Surely you ought to have brought a question of such delicacy to the Cabinet?"

Hobson paced about the room while the Prime Minister thought out his reply.

"It was for the very reason of its delicacy that I decided I

NUMBERS 10, 11, AND 12 DOWNING STREET

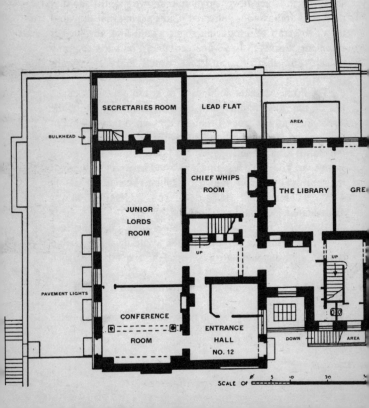

TERRA

SECRETARIES ROOM

LEAD FLAT

AREA

BULKHEAD

CHIEF WHIPS
ROOM

THE LIBRARY

GRE

JUNIOR

LORDS

ROOM

UP

UP

PAVEMENT LIGHTS

CONFERENCE

ROOM

ENTRANCE

HALL

NO. 12

DOWN

AREA

SCALE OF

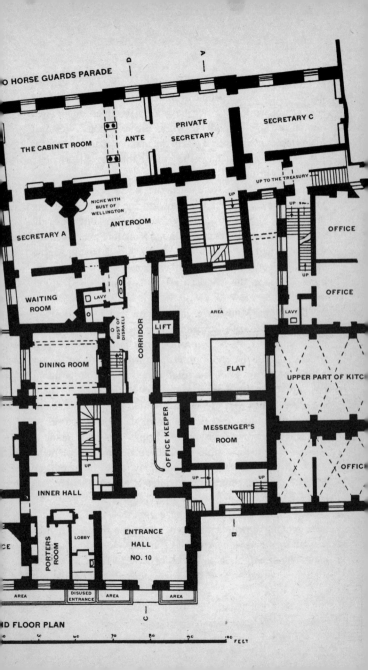

TO HORSE GUARDS PARADE

THE CABINET ROOM

ANTE

PRIVATE SECRETARY

SECRETARY C

NICHE WITH BUST OF WELLINGTON

ANTEROOM

UP

UP TO THE TREASURY

SECRETARY A

UP

OFFICE

WAITING ROOM

LAVY

BUST OF DISRAELI

OFFICE

UP

AREA

LAVY

CORRIDOR

LIFT

DINING ROOM

FLAT

UPPER PART OF KITC

MESSENGER'S ROOM

OFFICE KEEPER

OFFIC

UP

UP

INNER HALL

UP

PORTERS ROOM

LOBBY

ENTRANCE HALL

NO. 10

B

AREA

DISUSED ENTRANCE

AREA

AREA

C

ND FLOOR PLAN

FELT

should take the responsibility and I do. We have over two million unemployed people in this country right now – 10 per cent of our work force. We have an incredible trade deficit, our borrowings around the world are enormous. We must have employment, even if it is in the making of armaments for Israel. And we must have the dollars that the sale of those armaments brings in."

In a customary gesture to emphasize his point, the Prime Minister waved his left hand toward the Chancellor, slicing through the air in a slow, steady, forceful way. "But above all, under no circumstances is the United Kingdom to be ruled by, to be governed by, to be directed by the King of Saudi Arabia or the Sheik of Kuwait or any other money-stuffed and power-hungry ruler in the Middle East, or anywhere else for that matter!"

The Prime Minister, excited, stood and faced Hobson. "For Her Majesty's government to be hostage to, to be blackmailed by, to be controlled by a foreign government which has had the enormous good fortune to be sitting on billions of barrels of oil is a totally unacceptable proposition, not only to me, but I am sure to every British subject. There are some things that are more valuable than money, more valuable than jobs, and that is the right to govern ourselves and make our own decisions. As Prime Minister, I made a decision; I am responsible for it. Even if it means complete Arab withdrawal from our economy and the complete collapse and bankruptcy of the United Kingdom, it is a choice I believe the people of this country will support."

The Chancellor shifted his gaze from the Prime Minister's face, looking down at his own hands which were tightly pressed together, white knuckles showing. He nodded agreement. "You're right, Jeremy. You're perfectly right."

Sands turned and walked a few steps around behind his

desk, sat down, opened his black, tattered looseleaf work-book, and slipped on his reading glasses.

"Time is very short. We must have a plan of action. Every effort must be used to turn the Arabs around, at least to get some time to talk with them, to get them to change their minds." He picked up his desk pen. "Michael, in round figures, what do you estimate the amounts of the Arabs' straight bank deposits, the short-term deposits, in this country to be?"

Hobson sat down in front of the Prime Minister's desk and pulled a piece of paper from the inside pocket of his suit coat.

"I obtained that figure from the Deputy Governor of the Bank of England just before I left to come here. I got him out of bed, poor chap. The figures are appalling. He estimates 1.3 billion pounds in ordinary bank deposits that can be with-drawn at any time, another 3.5 billion pounds on very short-term deposit, that is, ten days or under, and another 23 billion in thirty- to sixty-day deposits, some of them longer in time. In 1974 alone, the OPEC* countries put in or through London 21 billion dollars of which a third was held in sterling. The problem is like that of the German banks that were caught while borrowing short-term from the Arabs but using that credit to lend long-term – that is, for a year, two, five, or more. Those banks were cut short when the Arabs pulled out their short-term money, and the banks had to go to the market to find 'roll-over' money, and couldn't do so. Our banks have been borrowing short and lending long also. In other words, when the Arabs try to withdraw their money from our banking system, as well as from the other U.K. depositories in which they've placed funds, there is no possible way they can be paid unless those banks can borrow from some other source. Normally, that other source is the Bank of England. But its reserves are low, less than three

* Organization of Petroleum Exporting Countries

billion pounds, and it has no further credit against which to borrow on the world market. As you know, Prime Minister, the Bank of England, with the approval of the Cabinet, has borrowed in the last two years twelve billion pounds in Euro-dollars, mainly from German sources. Like Italy, we had to pledge our gold reserves as a guarantee."

Hobson glanced at his notes once more, then returned them to his pocket. "So, the Bank of England is out of it and our banks and merchant banks have nowhere to turn to borrow funds to pay the Arab accounts," he said. "They might be able to find perhaps 20 per cent of the total indebtedness, around five billion pounds for the short-term deposits."

The Prime Minister took off his glasses, put down the pen, and leaned back in his chair. "How incongruous," he said, deep in thought. "The main cause of our trade deficit is that since 1973, when the Arabs and their partners upped their prices 400 per cent, we've been paying over eight billion dollars a year for their precious crude oil. It's what we have to pay them that has brought us to the point of bankruptcy. If only we had the North Sea oil in production now, we would be independent, self-sufficient in crude oil, and perhaps even exporters of oil." He shook his head sadly. "But the North Sea oil has only just started to come onshore. It's still two, three, perhaps four years away from significant production. And with the strikes we've had, the bottlenecks in the production of pipe-lining and pumping equipment and the floating drilling platforms, it may be five or ten years before oil flows in quantity from the North Sea. In any event, Michael, it's too late."

Pulling himself together, Jeremy Sands sat forward and picked up his glasses and pen. He began to write, speaking at the same time: "Steps to be taken – number one, the Foreign

Secretary must make immediate arrangements for me to fly to Riyadh to meet with the Saudis. Number two, the Chancellor of the Exchequer will immediately proceed to Washington to meet with the International Monetary Fund people and to attend upon the appropriate officials of the government of the United States to seek their assistance by direct loans, or their guarantee of the IMF, or the fund Kissinger got going – "

"Yes, the OECD* fund," Hobson interjected, "set up under the International Energy Agency. Might I respectfully suggest, sir, before either of the decisions you're talking about are taken that a meeting of the Cabinet be called. They should be briefed as to what has happened and why, and what you propose to do next."

The Prime Minister peered at the Chancellor over the glasses perched on the end of his nose. "Quite so, quite so. And as quickly as possible. Michael, be a good chap. Would you ring up the Foreign Secretary while I'm talking with the Secretary of the Cabinet. Get him over here as quickly as possible. You can use the telephone in the Green Room next door." Turning to pick up his own telephone on the credenza behind him, he went on, "And I'll get on to the Secretary of the Cabinet." He looked at his watch. "The Cabinet will meet at nine. Two hours, that should be enough notice."

The Prime Minister turned back toward the Chancellor as he was leaving the room. "And Michael, will you please be in touch again with the Bank of England. And you might also ring up the police. Just tell them there is a crisis developing to which I expect there will be enormous public reaction. Ask them to increase the security for 10 Downing Street to the maximum. Let Cutting know also."

Lord John Cutting was Sands' Secretary of Defence. Hobson nodded acknowledgement and left the room. The

* The Organization for Economic Co-operation and Development

21

Prime Minister found the private home number of the Foreign Secretary, Peter Stanton, in his special directory and dialled the number. To Sands' surprise, Stanton answered immediately. The Prime Minister quickly outlined the situation, his explanation being frequently interrupted by Stanton's questions.

"Now, Peter, here's what I want you to do – get on to the Prime Minister of Saudi Arabia. Ask him to delay the carrying out of their instructions to pull their money out of the U.K. for at least forty-eight hours, at least until I've had a chance to meet with my Cabinet and then meet with his King. Tell him I want to see the King and him as quickly as possible. I will fly out to Saudi Arabia today. Peter, do you think the Prime Minister will be offended if you speak to him and not I?"

"No, sir, I'm sure he won't. I've met him several times in the past few months. We get on very well. Like most of the ruling class in the Middle East, he was educated in Britain, University of Glasgow, I think. A very civilized chap. No, he won't take offence."

"Good. Ring me back as soon as you've talked with him. What time is it now in the Middle East, by the way?"

"There's one hour difference. They're Greenwich Mean Time plus three and we're plus two. I must say, sir, I hate to think of you having to go cap in hand to those people. It's bloody humiliating!"

The Prime Minister sounded as though he had given up. "I have no choice," he said. "I have absolutely no choice."

The Prime Minister had spoken without interruption from a single member of his Cabinet, a stunned and shocked group of men and women. He had briefed them thoroughly on the situation as he saw it: his secret authorization of the sale of the Rapier missiles to Israel, and the ramifications of the Arab withdrawal from the U.K. economy.

"Shortly after seven this morning, the Foreign Secretary spoke with the Prime Minister of Saudi Arabia and informed him that I was prepared to fly to the Middle East today to discuss the entire question with the King of Saudi Arabia and his people. On my instructions, the Foreign Secretary also asked that the execution of the decision to withdraw from the U.K. economy be delayed for forty-eight hours so we could talk with them and negotiate."

From his chair at the middle of the Cabinet table, Sands looked to his right and to his left at the faces watching him with apprehension. Then he glanced at the portraits of long-gone prime ministers that burdened the walls. In this room at the rear of 10 Downing Street, with its long, ancient, highly polished, paper-strewn Cabinet table, countless other crises and debates had taken place over innumerable decades. From

23

the peak of Britain's power to this, its abyss, decisions of enormous magnitude had been made here. But none seemed to equal those that would be made now and within the next two days. Sands turned to the Foreign Secretary sitting at his right. "Peter, perhaps you'd best say what the Saudi Prime Minister's answer was."

Stanton cleared his throat, then spoke hesitantly. "The Prime Minister of Saudi Arabia said that Britain had betrayed the Arab world, that Britain had disregarded the explicit instructions of Saudi Arabia, acting as the leader of the Arab world, when it secretly shipped the Rapier missiles to Israel. And that the government of Britain had done these things – had taken this step aimed at the heart of the Arab nations – notwithstanding the fact that the Arabs had been their friends for many decades and had invested billions upon billions of dollars in the United Kingdom. Then he said that for these reasons his King had instructed him that under no circumstances would the King be prepared to negotiate with or receive the Prime Minister of Great Britain; that notwithstanding the fact that the Arab action in withdrawing from the British economy would probably cost the Arabs ten to fifteen billion dollars in losses because the U.K. could not repay, the Arabs are prepared to make that sacrifice as an act of retribution. And that the decision to withdraw from the U.K. economy forthwith was irrevocable."

The Foreign Secretary paused and looked nervously toward the Prime Minister and around the table. He went on.

"He also said that if the U.K. banks and other depositories could not repay the Arabs on demand, which is what he fully expects, or if we cannot get loans from the United States or the International Monetary Fund or the OECD to cover the repayments to the Arabs – in other words, if Britain can't pay them and we're totally bankrupt – it also means they will no longer ship us crude oil."

The entire Cabinet, which had been listening in silence, erupted in bedlam.

The Prime Minister let it go on for a few moments, then did something he had never had to do before. He pounded the table for order. Once quiet had been restored, Sands started to speak when a new voice was heard.

"Haven't we got a contingency plan for just this kind of emergency – pre-arranged loans with the International Monetary Fund or the Americans?" demanded Agnes Potter, the Minister of the Environment. She was down the table on Sands' left. He could not see her, but her piercing, high-pitched voice identified her immediately.

The Chancellor of the Exchequer answered. "I asked the same question of the Bank of England this morning. Their answer was no."

Amid mutterings of alarm, Agnes Potter was insistent. "But what about you, Chancellor, have you a contingency plan?"

Hobson moved nervously. "We're working on one. My people should have something by mid-afternoon."

Agnes Potter pursued him further. "But you'll be in Washington by then. Prime Minister, it's almost impossible to believe there's no plan. I think the Chancellor ought to have had emergency arrangements organized for this very kind of situation."

On the defensive, the Chancellor fought back. "We have access to the IMF and the OECD funds! And who around this table expected, even gave one thought to the possibility the Arabs might pack it in?" No one responded to that challenge. "I've been on to the IMF but their director can't be reached. They expect to hear from him by eleven. I'll see him as soon as I get to Washington."

Sands intervened. "The fact is there is no plan. And at best we could get only five or six billion dollars out of the IMF – it

25

will take us a few days to make the arrangements. In the meantime, we must improvise and improvise quickly."

He went on. "This country is clearly facing the worst crisis in its history. Without money we cannot buy food, we cannot buy natural resources to feed our factories to make goods to sell to the world. We may not be able to borrow money because we have no credit. We have only roughly thirty days' supply of crude oil in storage and after that – " He threw up his hands in despair. "There are now over two million unemployed and by the end of this week probably another million. Crime and lawlessness are at unparalleled heights. Our unemployed are roaming the streets. There are demonstrations daily. When word of the Arab decision gets out today there will be a run on every bank in the country by people trying to get their savings out. The value of the pound sterling, which has already slipped to about two dollars, will probably be cut in half and more." Sands paused for a moment. "The simple truth is that we are indeed bankrupt. Britain is in a state of total economic collapse. And it is our responsibility – yours and mine."

There was a sharp response from the far end of the Cabinet table to his right. For a moment he was unsure of who had spoken.

"No, it's your responsibility, Prime Minister. If you hadn't authorized the sale of those bloody missiles to Israel this wouldn't have happened!"

It was Carter-Smith, the outspoken young left-wing Minister of Education and Science, a Trades Union Congress product whom Sands had been obliged, under heavy pressure from the TUC, to take into the Cabinet no more than a month before. To make matters worse from the P.M.'s point of view, Carter-Smith was from a well-to-do, upper-class family and had discovered socialism on his way through university. He was the worst kind of know-it-all radical. With his family fortune behind him, he was ready to redistribute everybody else's money among the workers. "Rather like a recent Canadian Prime Minister," Sands had been heard to comment.

Jeremy Sands' voice was cutting and sarcastic. "Mr. Carter-Smith, you're new around this table. If you'd had a bit more experience in government, you'd understand that my Rapier decision was merely the point that lanced a mountainous boil on the face of the British nation. Now the puss will flow. It will be a dreadful mess and it will take a long time to cure and be cleansed. But Britain will be cured and it will be cleansed! The collapse of our economy began a long time ago. The Rapier decision merely triggered the inevitable."

Sands' voice rose and his left hand lifted for a moment to make a punching, emphatic gesture down the length of the table toward Carter-Smith.

"Three major factors have brought Britain to this moment. The first and the most recent major blow to our economy was the Arabs' quintupling* – I'm sorry – the OPEC nations' quintupling of the price of crude oil during the 1971-75 period. Up until that time we were surviving. We were running a trade deficit, but it was of a size we could cope with. But by early 1974 we began to earn monthly trade deficits in the neighbourhood of one billion dollars, mainly because of the price of oil! Oil – a commodity for which we have no substitute – a commodity that is absolutely essential for the *physical* survival of our people, let alone the economic survival of the nation. And I might remind you, ladies and gentlemen," he said as he looked around the Cabinet table at his ministers, "I might remind you that the survival of this Government is now at stake."

* From $2.10 U.S. per barrel in 1971 to $10.90 in 1975.

Many of his colleagues shifted uncomfortably.

"Now, Mr. Carter-Smith," Sands went on vigorously, "the second major blow to our economy has been a long and steady one, which over the years has become a force-eight gale, spewing bankruptcies and corporate collapses everywhere. Moreover, it has literally killed the one human quality which when combined with industry could have put this country not in a trade deficit position, but in a surplus instead. That quality is something you seem to know little about Mr. Carter-Smith. It's called *productivity*!

"Productivity in Britain has been killed by the blow of irresponsible strikes promoted by ruthless trade unionists. In the pursuit of personal power they have embedded in the minds of the workers of this nation the concepts that all management is bad, all companies are corrupt, that profits grow on trees, and that the workers are entitled to their wages and to increasing wages regardless of whether they give a full day's work in exchange for a full day's pay. And for them the easiest way to get more money, more bread on the table, more of a share of the earnings, is not to increase productivity – heavens, that would be bad form – but to strike, to quit working, to stop producing, to shut the plant, to go on the comfortable dole and sing in one suicidal chorus, 'I'm all right, Jack, and anyway, the state owes me a living.' "

Carter-Smith tried to interject but the Prime Minister pressed on.

"I'm almost finished, but I want to make one thing clear. I am and always have been a supporter of our trade unions and of the principle that the workers of Britain are entitled to their fair share of earnings. My record is very clear. And I have always worked and this party has always worked in co-operation with the Trade Unions Congress. If the broad base of trade unions in Britain had been as responsible about strikes over the years as the TUC leadership wanted them to be and if they had put productivity ahead of strikes, then this country would be prosperous. Instead, it's bankrupt, mainly because the unions have taught the workers that to work is bad.

"There is one final factor – we have too many people on these Islands. If our people were as productive as they once were or as the Japanese are today, then numbers wouldn't matter. In my view, one of the decisions we have to come to grips with – a policy decision – is people. How can we get as many people as possible to get off the Islands, to migrate to Canada, the U.S., Australia, New Zealand, or wherever?

"But that is a matter we can discuss later in the day. What I want from all of you now is direction. Where do we go from here? How do we cope with the Arab pull-out? What should we be doing?"

The Cabinet meeting became tumultuous. Finally, the voice of Sir Benjamin Wicks, the diminutive Home Secretary, was heard above the uproar. Seething with indignation, he shouted to the Prime Minister. "We just can't take this lying down! The Arabs are not only cutting off their investments here, they're doing something even more damaging. They're cutting off our oil supply. Oil is absolutely essential for our industries' survival, and for that matter for our national survival. The Arabs are going to strangle us to death! The Americans have said that they would consider using force if they were being strangled by a major oil supplier. Well, we're being strangled. Aren't we justified in using force?"

The ministers looked expectantly at the startled Prime Minister. "Do you mean should we attack them, occupy them?" Sands finally asked.

"Yes, that's exactly what I mean!"

"You must be daft, Ben," said Lord Cutting. "This government has slashed my budget so badly I barely have the

29

strength to get a handful of ships to sea, a token number of fighters and bombers into the air, and enough troops to meet our home requirements, let alone NATO."

Wicks persevered. "Surely we could pull enough together for one big push. There are only a few countries to be taken – Saudi Arabia, Kuwait, the United Emirates – "

The Defence Secretary was emphatic. "Saudi Arabia itself has been arming rapidly. They've been buying fighter aircraft and ground-to-air missiles from the Americans. And their brother Arabs – Egypt, Syria, Iraq, and Jordan – are armed to the teeth – about a million troops, 1,500 fighter aircraft, over 6,000 tanks. Ben, there's no way.

"And even if we did have the military strength, neither the Soviets nor the U.S. and NATO would tolerate such action. The balance between the two sides is too delicate, particularly since American foreign policy collapsed in 1975. At one time I thought that the Russians and the Americans might hold each other off and not intervene if a strong bloc of western European nations went into the Middle East after the Arabs cut them off again. But for us to go it alone – it's inconceivable."

Sir Benjamin Wicks subsided.

As the session went on the staff of the Secretary of the Cabinet, Sir Peter Flood, carried a steady flow of messages to the appropriate ministers and took out written instructions for deputy ministers to implement. Shortly after 9:00 AM news of the Arab pull-out appeared on the wire services to newspapers, radio, and television stations across the country and the world. The radio and TV stations interrupted all programming to broadcast the calamitous news, often with panicky comment.

At 10:05 the Cabinet received word from the Governor of the Bank of England. His report was shattering. At the opening of trading in western Europe – Frankfurt, Paris,

Milan, Amsterdam, and Brussels – the pound had dropped in value from $2.107 U.S. (where it had closed the previous Friday) to $1.861, and was still sliding. The Arab instructions to their U.K. financial agents were being executed across the board. The selling off of shares had cut the *Financial Times* index in half from 149.5 to 73.6.*

Long queues of people were forming at every branch of every bank and savings depository. The citizens of the United Kingdom sensed the imminent collapse of the banking structure. They wanted their savings out of the banks and into their own hands. The people of Great Britain had joined the Arabs in what was the most disastrous run in history on the banking and financial system of any nation.

Moments before receiving the catastrophic news from the Bank of England, the Cabinet had resolved that "the Chancellor of the Exchequer be forthwith dispatched to the United States to urgently request that nation's immediate support by a direct loan of $25 billion together with that government's guarantee of loans from either the International Monetary Fund or the International Energy Agency's 'solidarity' fund." The latter had been set up during the Kissinger period to borrow Arab and OPEC money, some $25 billion at its outset in 1975, for recycling into the Western world's economy and for Third World nations hard hit by the earlier increases of OPEC crude oil prices.

It had also been decided that the Prime Minister would telephone his counterparts in West Germany and France asking for direct immediate loans from them to the maximum amount they could spare. Sands had been pessimistic about any approach to Europe because all U.K. credit had already

* Equivalent to a value of stock exchange quotations at about £42 billion; it peaked at £144 billion in 1972.

been used up in that market, but nevertheless he agreed to make the contacts.

Moreover, he undertook to talk with the President of the United States to brief him on the deteriorating situation and to plead for his personal involvement and assistance.

The Cabinet also decided that the Foreign Secretary should not attempt to contact the U.S. Secretary of State, who was in Moscow at that moment. The Prime Minister's approach to the President would be sufficient. The news of the gathering run on the banks made it imperative that the Chancellor be on his way to America immediately and that the appropriate contacts be made by the Prime Minister forthwith.

Just prior to leaving the meeting, the Prime Minister had a hurried private word with the Chancellor of the Exchequer before he departed for Washington. When Hobson left, the Prime Minister put before the Cabinet a mind-boggling proposal. Page ten of the Minutes of the Cabinet for that day recorded his motion in these words:

> The Prime Minister reviewed the dangers of the immediate withdrawal of savings funds from the banking and financial system, and the need to maintain a maximum degree of stability for at least seventy-two hours. He then moved and it was seconded and unanimously resolved that:
>
> 1) an Order-in-Council be and the same is hereby passed prohibiting any bank, trust company, or any other financial institution or the London Stock Exchange from transacting any business whatsoever until twelve o'clock noon (Double British Summer Time) of Thursday, the 8th day of July next; and
>
> 2) in anticipation of civilian disorders and for the purpose

of maintaining law and order during the aforesaid period that the Army and the Royal Air Force be so deployed as to provide immediate aid to the civil power if and when such assistance is requested or directed by the appropriate authorities.

10:16 AM London, England
4:16 AM Washington, D.C.

The Prime Minister placed his call to the President of the United States from the Secretary's office off the south side of the Cabinet Room. Sands had met President Sheppard several times and knew him well. At their first meeting in the early 1970's, Sands had been a junior minister with a trade mission to the United States, and the President had been one of the senators with whom the mission had met.

Daniel Sheppard had always been understanding and sympathetic about the U.K.'s mounting economic problems, but Sands had the feeling that the President – and for that matter all U.S. officialdom – looked down on Great Britain as a poor cousin who had fallen on hard times. The Brits were to be tolerated, but it was the Japanese and West Germans who were to be admired.

However, on this day the Prime Minister knew he had the President's full attention as he recited the facts. In his mind's eye Sands could see the tanned and fit President at his desk in the elegant Oval Office in his pyjamas and dressing gown, just as he himself had begun this day. The paunchy Sands, in his mid-sixties, had long envied the lean, athletic President who, in his late fifties, kept himself in top physical condition.

The telephone reception was clear and loud. The President had taken in the P.M.'s summary of the Arabs' action, the

34

initial loss in value of the pound, the actions of the British Cabinet, and the urgent need to borrow money not only to meet the pull-out demands of the Arabs but also to enable Britain to keep on buying crude oil.

After a series of probing questions followed by short, terse answers, the President said, "Okay, Jeremy, I've got all the basics. What a mess! You know we've had our share of troubles, too, and you know that Congress has been hand-cuffing me since the Watergate fiasco. But to the extent that I can commit the United States, I'll do everything in my power to see that we give Great Britain all the help we possibly can. Bear in mind, however, I've got real problems on the home front. The automotive industry is just getting up off its knees, and it's the heart of our economy. I've got six and a half million people unemployed,* although the situation's improving rapidly. Inflation has been knocking the hell out of us. Like you, we've been shipping our capital out to the OPEC countries, and in particular the Arabs, in order to buy their crude oil. I've got trade deficits like you have. But I think our economy has turned the corner. So what I'm saying is that I don't know how much direct help I can give you at this point, but I just want you to know that while we've got all kinds of problems ourselves, I for one will do everything I can to help. Having said that, what do you want us to do?"

The Prime Minister was a grateful man. "I can't tell you how relieved I am to have your assurance of support."

"Well, it all depends, Jeremy. Remember, I have severe limitations and a nervous Congress."

"Quite. Yes, I understand. No question about it. But your personal support will be of enormous assistance."

"Now, let me read part of a resolution that I presented to the Cabinet, and which was unanimously passed. The second

* 7.1% of the work force

35

part has to do with internal arrangements in the country, so I'll only read the part that refers to our approach to you for financial assistance or guarantee." The Prime Minister then quickly read the Cabinet motion directing the approach to the American government.

When the President heard the number, he practically shouted into the telephone. "Twenty-five billion! And you're also talking about an additional one billion a month to make up for the investment shortfall when the Arabs pull out, and you've got little or no prospect of overcoming your trade deficiency . . ."

"That's right, Mr. President. At least not until the North Sea fields are into full production."*

The President snorted, "In full production? My people tell me you're light years away from production. You got a trickle of oil flowing in by tanker during the summer of 1975. The trade unions have stopped the building of drilling platforms, the drilling operations, and the laying of pipe with one strike right after the other. And your government has insisted on taking at least a 51 per cent interest in all the fields. One of your principal oil companies, Burmah, has had to be bailed out by the Bank of England and taken out of the management position it had in the development of the oil fields. Our oil companies are prepared to take over management and clean that mess up for you, but your people just won't let go. If you gave the Americans a free hand at it, we'd have a million barrels of oil a day coming onshore within the next twenty-four months and enough to meet all your needs in the next two years . . ."

The Prime Minister broke in with his voice full of despair. "It's too late. It's just too late. I know all the things you're saying are true. We just can't put it together. If we had been

* 1975 estimates of reserves: 3 to 4.5 billion tons

able to we could have brought enough oil onshore to meet our needs. We would have had most of our trade deficiency beaten and we wouldn't be in this bloody mess."

"That's right," the President agreed. "You should have made it your national purpose to get that oil out and become self-sufficient. You should've passed every damn law and done everything that was absolutely necessary regardless! Instead you let the trade unions, inflation, and the lack of outside capital beat you." The President paused. He had hammered poor Sands hard enough on the point. There was nothing either one of them could do about it at that moment. "Okay, Jeremy, what do you want me to do now? You say Hobson's on his way across?"

"Yes, he's on his way to Heathrow Airport right now. If for any reason you can't see him or you think it's inadvisable for him to come, I could always stop him."

The President was emphatic. "No way. Let him come. The only concern I have is that the Secretary of State is in Moscow, scheduled to be back in Washington late tonight, although I may ask her to do something on the way home." He thought for a moment. "Doesn't matter. Let your Chancellor come. We'll meet with him as soon as we can. I'll have the key people in my Cabinet standing by."

The Prime Minister was grateful and relieved. "Excellent, Dan. I am very much obliged to you. If there are any problems or questions, I'll be available to you at all times."

"Good."

Sands went on. "As I told you, we're in Cabinet session here, and I expect we'll be at it most of the day as the scene shifts and changes. But there is one thing I would like you to think about. I haven't really raised it in Cabinet yet, but I'll do so shortly."

"What's that?"

"It's emigration, Dan. As your embassy people here have

probably reported to you, for the past month there have been hundreds of people lined up at your embassy, at the Canadian High Commission office, and at the Australian and New Zealand offices. With no jobs available and with an incredible number of people unemployed, the idea is 'get off the Islands.' With this disaster today, I can foresee that not only are we going to have an enormous number of people out of work, but we're going to have shortages of food as well. And what food there is will be priced so high that many people won't be able to buy it."

"So what are you getting at?" asked the President apprehensively.

"It's simply this. We had a Royal Commission study on emigration last year. Their estimate was that if the economy were to collapse about 10 per cent of our population would have to get off – will *want* to get off – the Islands within twelve months. Not only will they want to and have to leave, it is mandatory that we rationalize our population base – bring some balance between the number of jobs available and the population count. The economy will not support the population. So it's critical that we get a mass outflow of people going as quickly as possible. But until we know whether your people and Canada, Australia, and New Zealand will take them, we can't move."

There was a static interruption on the line which cleared as quickly as it came on.

The President was cautious. "I didn't quite get that, Jeremy. Did I hear you say 10 per cent?" he asked incredulously.

"That's right," Sands affirmed.

"But that's about six million people!"

"Precisely," the Prime Minister agreed. "And many of them will want to go to the United States. The emigration statistics show us that about a third will want to go the States . . ."

"You mean, two million people? In a year?"

"Yes, two million people in a year, and possibly more. It might even be less than a year, depending on what happens in this country. Two million to Canada and the rest to Australia and New Zealand. We have no choice, Dan. We've got to help these people get out. I'm going to make a proposal to Cabinet shortly as to policy and mechanics. And if Cabinet agrees, I'll be back to you to ask you and Congress to open the gates to America."

10:29 AM
The Cabinet Room
10 Downing Street
London, England

As he entered the Cabinet Room from the Secretary's office, the Prime Minister stopped short in surprise. The tumultuous Cabinet he had left a few minutes earlier was at this moment sitting in total silence, stunned into speechlessness by what they had just heard. Standing at the far end of the long table was Sir Richard Pilling, the Governor of the Bank of England.

The Prime Minister asked in a loud voice, "What is it, Sir Richard? What's happened now?"

The Governor spoke slowly, an ominous tone in his voice. "Prime Minister, the decision of the Cabinet to close all banking, coupled with the Arab withdrawal, has meant that the City of London ceased to be the world's main international banking centre and exchange as of this hour. The result of the action of the Cabinet – and I respectfully point out, Prime Minister, that I was not consulted in this action – has been to stop all monetary transactions, not only domestic, which was undoubtedly in your mind, but even more important, all, and I mean all, international transactions. In one stroke you have reduced the Bank of England and the entire banking system of this nation to nothing more than a national system, nothing more, nothing more. The flow through all our clearing banks – Barclays, Lloyds, Midland, Nat West – of world monies, world currencies, whether marks, francs, Petro-dollars, Euro-dollars or whatever, has totally stopped. All confidence is lost, and the pound has already suffered an enormous run."

The Governor looked away from the Prime Minister, down the table at the transfixed Cabinet.

"What I had just finished telling your colleagues, Prime Minister, was that when the banks are again open for business whenever it is you in fact decide they should reopen – I understand it's next Thursday – I predict you will find the value of the pound to be in the range of not two dollars U.S. as it was at the close of trading last Friday, or $1.60 as it is now, but one dollar or less. And you will also find, sir, that all of the reserves of the Bank of England will be used up not in attempting to meet the Arab pull-out of their deposits, but in meeting the ordinary citizen who will want in the most desperate way to get his money out of the bank or near-bank which holds his money."

The Prime Minister protested. "But we had no choice but to shut down the banking system. The run on the banks which was obviously beginning . . ."

Sir Richard Pilling looked the Prime Minister squarely in the eye. He spoke coldly, bitterly. "Sir, I have been the Governor of the Bank of England for twelve years. And during that period of time I have served six governments – two of yours including this one. I believe I have served you and them well. I had a contingency plan for exactly this kind of situation, a situation which has been totally predictable whatever the trigger. My plan was designed to meet a domestic run by supporting the banks with the Bank of England's existing reserves, together with funds, five billion dollars, that I had arranged some three months ago with the Director of the International Monetary Fund to which you are

41

now planning to go. I had made those arrangements subject to the necessary Cabinet approval should an event of this kind occur."

"So we can draw on the IMF immediately. Is that what you're saying?"

"You could have, Prime Minister, and you could have kept your domestic banks in operation. But it's too late now you've closed the banks. Because of this I'm sure the IMF will want to review the commitment they gave to me."

Sands was indignant. "Why didn't you tell us you had made the IMF arrangement?"

"There was no need to unless an emergency arose. It arose and you did not seek my advice. The result is twofold, Prime Minister. Disaster for our economy and our banking system and disaster for sterling. My resignation as the Governor of the Bank of England, sir, has already been lodged with the Secretary of the Cabinet."

"Wait one minute," the Prime Minister replied. "Surely the Chancellor has been in discussion with you right through this whole piece. Surely you would have told him about your contingency plan when he talked with you this morning after his meeting with me?"

"He did not speak with me, Prime Minister. He spoke with my deputy. Everyone in this room knows the Chancellor and I have been at loggerheads for the past year after I was quoted as contradicting a policy statement he had made. So far as I'm concerned, you've got a fool for a Chancellor. Now that I've resigned, I intend to say so publicly and loudly!"

His mouth agape, the Prime Minister watched his former Governor of the Bank of England leave the Cabinet Room. As the door shut behind him, the Prime Minister turned, moved to his chair in front of the fireplace, and slumped into it. His eyes were vacant as his brain concentrated on sorting out the ramifications of the Governor's resignation and the enormity of the tactical error that had been made as a result of the animosity between the Chancellor and the Governor of the Bank of England. Sheer stupidity. But as Prime Minister, it was Sands' responsibility and he would have to bear it.

"Prime Minister?" Sands could barely hear the voice asking for his attention. A little louder the next time. "Prime Minister?" This was a Scottish voice he recognized all too well, with its lilting, light burr and acid sharpness. It belonged to Angus M. Stewart of Glasgow, the leader of the Scottish nationalists in the House of Commons. With their growing numbers in the House, Sands had been reluctantly forced to recognize their position and weight. With a minority government after the last election, he had negotiated a coalition with Stewart's group of fifteen Scots in exchange for two Cabinet appointments, one for Angus Stewart, the other for his deputy leader, Margaret Wright from Aberdeen. Stewart was the Minister of State in the Scottish Office and Wright now held the portfolio of Minister of Health and Social Security.

Notwithstanding Stewart's presence in the Cabinet, the Prime Minister and he could barely abide each other. For Stewart, the Prime Minister embodied everything that he hated in the English: massive power, oppression of the poor, and particularly the holding down of the Scots. And for Sands, Stewart was the personification of racism, wild-eyed nationalism, and irresponsible claims for self-government, in particular for Scottish ownership of North Sea oil.

Stewart sat on the opposite side of the Cabinet table to the Prime Minister, at the end of the table to his right. The Scotsman now had Sands' full attention.

The burr grated on Sands' ears. "Prime Minister, d'ye know what some of us got to be thinking about at this moment? I suppose not. Let me tell ye. It won't take but a wee while." Suddenly his Glasgow usage gave way to his Cambridge University background. The English flowed

43

smoothly, eloquently, and without a trace of Scottish accent. "I think all of us here have been witness this morning to a classic demonstration of political and leadership ineptitude of the first order."

Sands looked intently at Stewart, whose jet-black beard jumped as he went harshly on through the cries of "Shame, shame" from the Prime Minister's own people.

"First you tell us you approved the Rapier sale to the Israelis on your own responsibility without reference to this Cabinet and you did so for reasons of security. At least that's why you say you didn't bring it to the Cabinet. You made your decision because to do otherwise would be an infringement on our sovereignty by the Saudis. And so far as I'm concerned, you made the decision knowing that if the Arabs found out – or better still, *when* they found out – the possibility, yes, the probability that the Arabs would do exactly as they have done was very high." Stewart's voice rose. His piercing dark brown eyes flashed. "That was a judgement, sir, which no individual ought to have taken alone under any circumstances, regardless of what you call the need for secrecy and security. The result of your arrogant act, Prime Minister, has brought this country to a state of total economic collapse. All in the name of sovereignty."

The Prime Minister protested. "Now see here – "

But Stewart would not be stopped. "And then having brought us this far, and with some prospect of salvation available through the foresight of the Governor of the Bank of England, we are treated to the astonishing spectacle of your Chancellor refusing to talk to the Governor when it was clearly his duty. If he had followed your instructions, Prime Minister, the United Kingdom would have a way out. As it is, the two of you have brought down not only your precious England, but our beloved Scotland as well, and I say, Prime Minister, that you ought to resign!"

44

This demand brought the members of the Cabinet to their feet. Shouts of "No, no!" and "Resign yourself, you swine!" could be heard above the pounding of the Cabinet table and the general agitation. Fists were brandished vigorously at Stewart, who remained, with Margaret Wright, seated and silent, as did the Prime Minister himself.

Sands, at the middle of the table, fought to control his emotions. He longed to stand up and shout with his colleagues, to make threats, to protect his honour, his actions, and his position, in as violent and forceful a way as he could. But during his long years in politics, Jeremy Sands had been berated by the best. Only once had he fallen into the trap when a sharp-tongued, wicked-mouthed old harridan carved him up at the end of his speech at an important party convention. Never again would he give in to the temptation, although Stewart's bilious invective brought him within a stroke of counterattack.

Instead the Prime Minister sat back, watching his colleagues and listening patiently. Slowly he pulled out his ancient, ash-beaten, smelly pipe, which still had some useable tobacco in it, tamped it, then lit it with deliberate movements.

Gradually the din died down; the ministers resumed their seats, still muttering. The two closest to Stewart and Wright moved their chairs away, isolating the Scottish nationalists. When the noise subsided the Prime Minister took the pipe from his mouth, laid it on the Cabinet table, and spoke just loudly enough for his voice to be heard.

"Mr. Stewart, I must confess I recognize some validity in the accusations you make. To argue otherwise is not possible. In making the decision on the Rapier missiles with all the attendant risks, I decided in favour of the need to preserve the integrity, the soul of my country, my nation. Above all others in this room, you who have a strong patriotic feeling for Scotland well understand what I am saying. Indeed, I'm sure

45

you'd be more than prepared to take comparable risks for Scotland."

Stewart made no response, not a flicker of emotion on his craggy face.

The Prime Minister went on. "As to the actions of the Chancellor in not dealing with the Governor, this I find totally unacceptable. I can understand in human terms how it happened, but the consequences are beyond belief. As Prime Minister, the responsibility is mine, just as the responsibility for the Chancellor's failure to have an emergency plan is mine also."

Sands reached into his left trouser pocket, extracted his handkerchief, blew his nose vigorously, put the handkerchief back, and continued.

"It did not escape my attention, Mr. Stewart, that when you so eloquently called for my resignation, you abstained from threatening to resign yourself should I fail to step down and make way for someone else at this table." Some heads nodded in approval and recognition of this point. "Furthermore, I believe you have no intention whatsoever of resigning from this Cabinet at this moment, regardless of how you feel about me. You are either too selfish, or too anxious to retain a position of power at this time of crisis, or you have a strong sense of duty not only toward your own people and Scotland, but as well to the United Kingdom and the Queen."

This brought a reaction from Stewart, but Sands would not let him intervene. "Frankly, Mr. Stewart, I don't give a damn what your motivation is. The fact is you're not about to resign because you know as well as I do the last thing this country needs is for this Cabinet to be split, or for this government to resign."

There were several shouts of "Hear, hear" around the table.

"And I can tell you that until a majority, yes, perhaps not

46

even a majority but a significant number of my own colleagues around this table have lost confidence in me and do express themselves accordingly, there is no possible way I will resign and walk away from the responsibility which the people of this country and my party have given me."

Stewart sat tight lipped as the Prime Minister's statement was roundly applauded by energetic thumping of the Cabinet table. The Prime Minister picked up his pipe, lit it again, puffed away a few times, then announced, "I think it would be appropriate to have a short break so each of you can check with your staff people. We'll reconvene in twenty minutes. We'll have lunch here in the dining room. I suggest that if you have any engagements for the rest of the day or this evening, you cancel them. We will remain in session to cope with each situation as it arises. If we do break off at any time, I want all of you to be available to reconvene at a moment's notice."

The Prime Minister stood up. "And when we reconvene after this break, one of the main items I want to deal with is the question of getting as many people as we can off these Islands as soon as possible."

The Secretary of State of the United States of America looked intently into the mirror of the sumptuous, spacious principal bedroom of the U.S. Embassy in Moscow. The final touches of makeup were applied to the slight pouches under the eyes. At the age of fifty-one, the Secretary was concerned about certain lines that were beginning to deepen.

She needed a rest. Three weeks would be heaven. But where would the Secretary of State of the United States find three weeks for a vacation, or to do anything by herself – or with her husband for that matter. It was not possible. Once you take on the job, it is twenty-four hours a day. The President had warned her almost a year ago when he invited her to take the position. "Jessica," he had said, "it's a twenty-four-hour-a-day job simply because the interests of the United States are worldwide economically, geopolitically, and militarily. At this moment in Japan, Vietnam, South Korea, North Korea, in India, China, the Soviet Union, Australia, you name it, in practically every country of the world, there are events happening, and people making them happen, that we're interested in. The State Department with the assistance of the CIA monitors the world. Your job would be to sit on top of that world and to speak for me and, therefore, the United

States. But, Jessica, if you take the job, and I know you will, both you and your husband must understand that the time commitment is total. There will be no time for vacations, no time really for anything except the affairs of the United States of America.''

How right the President had been. State had consumed her. In fact, the last time she had been home was over a month ago. She thought of a news report she had read some years before about a bachelor member of the British House of Commons who complained that he spent so much time sitting on committees, attending the House, and carrying on his business, that it was interfering with his sex life. She had laughed at the time. Now it was no joke.

Jessica Swift finished her makeup job to her satisfaction. She was ready for the Soviets, and experience told her they would be ready for her.

The Secretary did a final check on her dress as she stepped in front of the full-length mirror in the bathroom. She was a tall woman, just a touch under five feet nine, and really taller than she would have elected to be if she had had a choice. Her body was trim, tending toward a slinky thinness. Her elegant carriage was the result of a young girl's countless hours of practice in ballet. Her face, long and angular to match her body, was topped by a rich flow of black hair, which she had learned to coif and take care of herself. There was just no time to get to a hairdresser. Arched eyebrows set off large, inquisitive, intelligent, brown eyes. Her long nose had just a slight hook in it, a hand-me-down from her father. Her mouth and full lips were more often than not turned up in a smile, displaying even white teeth which contrasted with a clear, almost swarthy skin, another gift from her Lebanese father, Youssef Salloum.

Her intelligence and wit, combined with her learned academic background as one of America's foremost political scientists and lecturers, had earned her the offer of the post of Secretary of State. She had specialized in foreign affairs as a professor at Columbia University, where she had later become the chairman of the department. Her several books on foreign relations and many papers on that and interrelated subjects had taken her to national prominence by her mid-forties. Her name was at the top of a very short list of candidates the President had been given when the time had come to find a new Secretary of State. The President, being a very conservative man, had made enquiries about the status of her marriage and was pleased when he was advised that every indication was that her relationship with her husband, Donald Swift, now a senior banker with Chase Manhattan, was solid and stable. Theirs had been a late marriage, both being then in their middle forties. There were no children to encumber her movements should she accept the President's offer, which of course she did with the full blessing and understanding of her husband.

The President had had only one reservation about her appointment. Donald Swift was Jessica's second husband. In her early twenties, while still at university taking her master's degree in political science, she had married one of her teachers, a man twenty years her senior. Within a year they had broken up. From that time until she had met Donald Swift, Jessica had "played the field." As a fully liberated woman she had taken on a series of men and had been quite open about her relationships with them.

It was just this aspect that had concerned the President. Obviously Jessica Swift had a high interest in men. She was an extraordinarily attractive woman. There would be pressures on her in the Secretary's job, temptations, the possibility of being caught if she weakened. The Russians were renowned for luring important persons into compromising sexual situations, then using photographic evidence to blackmail. The

Soviets had no monopoly on this primitive, powerful technique. Would Jessica Swift be able to resist the male temptations which were bound to be placed in her path? An FBI check confirmed that since her marriage to Swift there was no evidence of any straying. And so the President had put aside his reservation and offered her the post.

The telephone beside her bed rang. Her self-inspection completed, she moved out of the bathroom to answer the call. She was a little startled to find it was the President himself on the line. A glance at her watch and a quick calculation told her it was only 4:35 AM in Washington. Something important must be up for Sheppard to be calling direct at this early hour.

"Jessica?"

"Yes, Mr. President. What in heaven's name are you doing up at this hour of the morning? It's only 4:35 your time, assuming you're in Washington."

"Yes, I'm in Washington, Jessica. In my pyjamas and dressing gown, in the Oval Office. I must be quite a sight. I've just had a call from Jeremy Sands . . ." The name conjured up pleasant memories and thoughts in the Secretary's mind. One of her favourite people in the world, a "super guy," as she sometimes described him. The President went on. "He's got real problems." The President described the conversation he had with Sands a few minutes before. Sitting on the edge of the bed with a pad and pen she had fished out of her purse, Jessica scribbled furiously, making notes of what the President was saying. "I've agreed to meet the Chancellor of the Exchequer, what's his name?"

"Hobson."

"Yes, Hobson. He's flying across today but I really don't want to meet him until you're here, sweetheart." The President had the unshakeable habit of calling ladies of whom he was fond "sweetheart." The Secretary of State was no exception. "And by the way, why are you in Moscow? I just can't keep up with you."

"What do you want first? My plans or why I'm in Moscow?"

"It's my nickel. Try why you're in Moscow."

They both laughed lightly.

"I'm in Moscow for a MEAL talk."

The President remembered. "Ah, yes. The Middle East Arms Limitations."

"Exactly." Some weeks before, the Secretary had gone to the President with a proposal that she be authorized to open negotiations with the Soviet Union for the purpose of working out a formula under which they would both agree to limit their arms sales to Middle East countries. The United States was, of course, in a peculiar position inasmuch as it supplied aircraft and weapons to Saudi Arabia as well as to Israel, the blood-enemy of the Arabs, and also to the Shah of Iran. The Soviets, on the other hand, were supplying Egypt and Syria, while the French, with their close Arab ties and high dependency upon Arab oil, sold their aircraft wherever they could in the Arab world, but not to the Israelis.

For the American manufacturers of fighters and helicopters, and the instrumentation and equipment that go into them, the Middle East market was a major bonanza. For the American economy generally, it was an excellent way to recycle some of those elusive Petro-dollars back into the Western economy. The Arabs and Iranians would order billions of dollars worth of U.S. aircraft and spare parts, which would create jobs, thousands upon thousands of jobs, all across the country. When the aircraft were produced, they would then be shipped out to the Middle East, where sooner or later they would be used in one of those inevitable wars; whereupon the Arabs would spend more Petro-billions to buy replacement aircraft.

For a suffering American economy with millions of jobless and billions of dollars being transferred out of the Western economic system into the hands of the Arabs and OPEC countries for crude oil, the need to recycle those Petro-dollars was of critical importance. The sale of aircraft and other armaments to the Middle East was a significant development. It was also a development that could not be tampered with without raising the ire of congressmen, aircraft and other armaments manufacturers, the Pentagon, and the labour unions.

The British had been selling tanks and ground-to-air missiles in the Middle East but not in any large numbers. The Secretary knew that the British had been instructed by the Arabs not to sell any further armaments to Israel, but, knowing Sands, she had doubted that he would accept that Arab infringement on the sovereignty of the United Kingdom.

Notwithstanding these strong pressures, the President was deeply concerned about the morality of selling these costly weapons of death to the oil-rich Middle East nations dedicated to the obliteration of a people within their region. Indeed, if the combined Arab forces did in the future overpower Israel, it would be likely that the United States would have to move in to protect the people of Israel from being massacred by their dedicated blood-enemies. What the Germans did to the Jews in the years preceding and during the Second World War would not compare in any way to the mass extermination of all the people in Israel. Should such an event happen, the United States would in the President's mind be culpable, having supplied much of the armament. He found this possibility distasteful. The actions of the United States in selling this lethal weaponry indiscriminately to Arabs and Israelis alike was against the spirit of the Constitution and all the things the United States stood for. And the

Vietnamese and Cambodian disasters were still fresh in everyone's mind.

Consequently, the President had approved Jessica Swift's proposal that exploratory talks be opened with the Soviet Union to determine whether there was a mutual ground of concern. If there was, then the two major world powers would move toward establishing a basic formula whereby each would agree to limit its sales. Once a fundamental accord was reached between them, they could attempt to influence France, Great Britain, and West Germany to join them.

This was the first MEAL meeting. The Soviets attached importance to it because the Chairman of the Supreme Soviet, Yaroslav, was to be present at the luncheon at which Secretary Swift was was due at twelve o'clock, and he was to attend the meeting that afternoon. Jessica had been informed that the subject matter was only one of the reasons that Yaroslav wanted to attend. The other was that Jessica Swift was to be present, and he was an admirer of the handsome Secretary of State.

"My plans so far, Mr. President, are these. I go to the luncheon hosted by Yaroslav at twelve noon, that is, within the hour. The first MEAL session begins at two. I will be airborne by seven this evening, direct for Washington. I have a staff meeting organized for tomorrow morning at ten at Foggy Bottom, and I have to fire, with your approval of course, our ambassador to Japan. He's been drinking too much and spending too much time in the Japanese baths. I see him at 11:30."

"Are you using the 747 Air Force One for this trip?"

"Yes, Mr. President, I am."

"You know, if you don't stop using that airplane, I'm going to have to start taking commercial airlines to get around the country."

Jessica laughed. "Yes, and you'll have to go tourist class."

"I may have to do just that," the President replied. Then his tone changed. "I'd like you to cancel your plans for tomorrow, Jessica. When you leave Moscow, go direct to Saudi Arabia and see the King. See if you can talk him into backing off his hard-line, anti-British position. Tell him he's going to bankrupt the U.K. and destroy the British international banking system, and he may well plunge the whole of the economy of Europe into a depression. You know what to say to him as well as I do. The aim is to do everything you can to get him to reverse his position."

"Right, I'll do that. Assuming the King will see me, I'll meet with him tomorrow morning. Subject to disasters and calamities, I would hope to be out of Riyadh after lunch, which should put me into Washington around six or seven tomorrow night."

"Okay, sounds good. I'll delay the meeting with the Chancellor until you get back. Now, sweetheart, don't have too many vodkas with the Russians. After all, I don't want them drinking you under the table . . ."

Jessica Swift couldn't resist the temptation. "Or into bed?"

12:00 NOON
The Cabinet Room
10 Downing Street
London, England

During the Cabinet break Sands had talked with the Queen and the Prince, both of whom had expressed grave concern about the Arab action, the collapse of the British pound sterling, and the future of the nation. Sands had attempted to reassure them about their own personal safety and the security of their position, but such assurances were unnecessary. The Queen simply took the position that she and her family were in fact the servants of the people. She asked the Prime Minister to advise the Cabinet that they would be available to him and his colleagues by telephone or in person, at any time during the crisis.

By the time Sands had finished his discussion with the Queen, his principal secretary had found the Prime Minister of Canada, Joseph Roussel, in Kuwait. Roussel was in the middle of a money-borrowing and identity-making tour of the principal oil-producing countries of the Middle East, cap-in-hand, hoping to lay the groundwork for better recognition by Saudi Arabia, Kuwait, Abu Dhabi, and Qatar. The Shah of Iran was not as difficult, since Canada had posted an ambassador in Teheran for many years. However, the Canadian government had ineptly and short-sightedly accredited that ambassador to the Arab countries, failing to recognize the long-standing antipathy between Iran and the Arab nations, and the fact that the Arabs were Arabs and the Iranians were Persians. As a result, when Arab oil-producing nations were becoming enormously rich through the sale of their oil and were accumulating massive surplus monies for investment capital, which a developing country like Canada needed in enormous quantities, Canada had no presence or stature with the Arabs.

As the staggering scale of the capital needs of Canada to the year 2000 had become known to Joseph Roussel (for example, $250 billion for energy and energy-associated projects alone – for the Mackenzie Valley pipeline, the James Bay Project, nuclear power plants, Athabasca Tar Sands, development of the gas and oil fields in the Mackenzie delta and in the Arctic Islands, and a host of other projects) it had become crystal clear that the Canadian federal government would have to join the homage-paying groups who were going to the Middle East to gain the favour and confidence of the sheiks, the ruling Arab families, and the Shah of Iran. So the Prime Minister of Canada had gone on the Middle East circuit with his Minister of Finance, André Vachon, and Roussel's principal secretary, Pierre Pratte.

When Sands attempted to phone him, Roussel and his colleagues were at the Royal Palace closeted with the Kuwaiti ruler and his senior ministers; he could not be reached. Sands asked that Roussel be given a message asking him to call on a matter of great urgency. He had then returned to the Cabinet Room where the emergency crisis session had resumed. Within an hour the Cabinet had dealt with a wide range of emergency proposals.

Without unanimity on any point and after heated discussion on each issue, some of the most drastic measures ever invented by a British government were decreed: rationing by coupon of all imported foodstuffs; similar rationing of all petrol and a cutback of 25 per cent on all imports of crude oil; control and limitation of the importation of all commodities, with a complete ban on all "luxury" items; all wages and prices were frozen and the marginal income tax rate on all incomes above £10,000 a year was set at 100 per cent."

During the debate about the crude oil cutback, Carter-Smith pointed out that the Arabs had already made the decision for the U.K. by cutting off not only their investments but their supply of oil as well.

The Prime Minister acknowledged the obvious, saying, "This is one of the critical questions Hobson will be taking up with the President and his Cabinet. Even if we can get an alternate source of supply, how are we going to pay for it? We're going to have to rely on the Americans to bail us out on this one."

"Or the Shah of Iran," added Malcolm Ross, Sands' Secretary of Energy. He sat opposite the Prime Minister at the Cabinet table. "I think, Prime Minister, that we ought to be making overtures not only to the Americans but to the Shah as well. He gave us a loan of 1.2 billion dollars in 1974 – it's in good standing. His oil production is now up to seven million barrels a day. And he is friendly to Great Britain, always has been."

Sands agreed. "No question about it. We should be talking with him."

"*You* should be talking with him, Prime Minister," Ross insisted. "He wouldn't deal with any lesser member of the Cabinet. And you won't be able to negotiate with the Shah by telephone. You'll have to attend upon him in Teheran."

"I suppose you're right. But if I go anywhere right now, it should be to the United States first. Hobson can probably carry it off over there by himself, but my instinct tells me I should go to Washington."

Ross nodded his accord as did several other ministers. From the end of the table came Stewart's voice again.

"I agree with the Energy Secretary. After hearing how Hobson botched up matters with the Bank of England I think you've sent a fool to Washington. Prime Minister, I think it's imperative that you go to Washington immediately."

The Prime Minister looked around the table at his colleagues to assess their reaction. Clearly there was a consensus that he should go.

"Very well. I shall go. But not until tomorrow morning. There are just too many decisions to be taken here today. It's impossible to tell what's coming next. I will leave Heathrow at 7:00AM. Lord John, could you make the necessary arrangements with the Queen's Flight, please?"

Lord John Cutting, the Secretary of State for Defence, sitting two places to the left of Sands, acknowledged the request.

Sands added, "I will go from Washington direct to Teheran, that is if the Shah will receive me." He turned to his Foreign Secretary across the table and asked, "Peter, would you be good enough to make the necessary arrangements through our ambassador in Teheran. Ask him to inform the Shah that I will let him know my arrival time as soon as I can, probably it will be late Wednesday or early Thursday. And would you get on to the President's people to make arrangements there. And let Hobson know I'm coming."

"I shall," Stanton responded. He left the Cabinet Room immediately.

The Prime Minister continued. "Now, before we break for lunch, I want to raise the matter of emigration, which I consider to be of the utmost urgency and concern. We have been looking at this crisis really only in terms of economics, money, jobs, rationing. We haven't really yet talked about people and the effects on them, on the family, on the individual. It is clear to me on this emergency crisis day our people are going to face unemployment on an unparalleled scale. Certainly it is not unreasonable to expect there will be factory shutdowns across the country. We'll have an unemployment figure of close to three million almost immediately. No jobs will mean no money, and with the state of the treasury at this moment the ability of the government to pay unemployment benefits will be limited to two or three weeks before our reserves are exhausted. So in all likelihood, we'll have literally millions of people without money to buy food, to pay rent, to keep up their never-never payments – assuming, that is, that we work out another part of this crisis, which is how to keep crude oil flowing into this nation.

"Every reading I can get, ladies and gentlemen, is that with the collapse of our ability to pay for our imports – that's where we've arrived right now – this country is going to be faced with enormous shortages. I'm sure that countries like the United States and Canada and Australia will not let our people starve. But the fact is we're going to be in a dreadful position for the foreseeable future."

Stanton quietly entered the Cabinet Room and resumed his seat. The Prime Minister went on.

"My information is that even before this day the number of emigration applications made and current in the hands of all four of the English-language countries is approximately 700,000. It is not unreasonable to expect that as of today literally millions of Britons will want to get off the Islands. Furthermore, I think it should be policy that they should get off and as quickly as possible. In fact, I consider it a matter of extreme urgency that we create a policy of emigration assistance for up to 10 per cent of our population, roughly six million people – the number estimated by the Royal Commission a year ago. By assistance, I mean government payment of air and sea passage, contribution to their maintenance for a period of, say, two years, and the establishment of offices to assist these people in making their applications to the countries of their choice."

"Do you really think the Americans will take any at all?" asked Environment Minister Agnes Potter. "They're just coming out of a severe recession. Their unemployment situation has been bad. The auto industry's been in a slump. Really, Prime Minister, I think you're optimistic."

"Perhaps I am, Agnes, but the question is should we adopt an open-gate emigration policy. If we agree on that point – and I detect that no one around this table's going to oppose it – then we speculate about whether the United States or Canada or Australia and New Zealand will take our people, or whether we have to take action to open their gates to them."

Sands looked at each of his colleagues around the table. "Does anyone have any comment on this proposal?"

"Just one, Prime Minister." It was Carter-Smith again. "I think we should have done this a long time ago." There were mutters of agreement.

"Perhaps," Sands responded. Then, satisfied that there was agreement he said, "It would appear that the open-gate emigration policy is acceptable to Cabinet. Now, let's get on to the question of our chances in getting the English-language countries to take our people.

"You should know that I've already opened the matter with the President. I think I shocked him pretty badly. The best I can say is that he didn't say yes or no. In any event, he's already considering the problem. I told him that if Cabinet approved of the open-gate policy I would get back to him. I'll do that personally at our meeting tomorrow."

Sands motioned in the direction of Peter Stanton saying, "The Foreign Secretary and I have been looking at this matter for some time now. We perceive the prime difficulty in

61

the United States, where stringent quotas exist on immigration, and in Canada, where they have a point system.

"Peter, would you please tell us about the real snags as you see them, particularly in the United States and Canada?"

Stanton slipped on his half-glasses and pulled out a sheet of paper from the file on the Cabinet table in front of him. "I will deal with Canada first. Canada has just enacted new immigration legislation. They produced a Green Paper back in 1975 which was intended to and in fact did form a basis for a national debate on the direction in which the country should be going. There was alarm that immigration was increasing so rapidly that it was getting out of hand. In 1974 they had over 200,000 people go into the country. In 1975, faced with high unemployment just as we were faced with it, a decision was made to attempt to keep immigration down to that number – 200,000 people. To do this, the Canadian government, which used the point system, changed its regulations to penalize prospective immigrants ten points if they did not have prearranged jobs in Canada, or the skills to hold positions in worker-scarce areas. Under the Canadian point system, an applicant needs fifty of a possible one hundred points to gain admission as a landed immigrant.

"The key issue is that the Canadian government wants to keep the immigration level at no more than 200,000. This is reflected in the new legislation which has just been passed, so it is now definite policy. A major concern in Canada is that some 55 per cent of the immigrants go to the three major Canadian metropolitan centres: Toronto, Montreal, and Vancouver, even though job opportunities are better in other parts of the country. Even so, the government in its new legislation does not impose an 'indenture' system, by forcing immigrants to live in particular areas.

"Another concern is that only a small number of immigrants settle in the French-Canadian province of Quebec.

Most of them head for Ontario. In fact, in 1972 when immigration was only 122,000, one-half went to Ontario, 20,000 to British Columbia, and only 19,000 to Quebec.

"The major stumbling block to a mass movement of people from our country into Canada is, of course, Quebec. The French-Canadians in that French-language province are greatly concerned that as the population of what they call English Canada keeps growing and overpowers them, they will lose their language and their culture. In fact the move toward separation or independence for Quebec has been very strong for the past two decades. It is likely that if the Canadian government were to consider the question of letting in say two million people from the United Kingdom, it would probably crystallize the Quebec threat of separation. There is no doubt in my mind that Quebec would fight tooth and nail against an influx of Britons on the mass scale of, say, two million.

"Another factor to be considered is that English Canada is no longer British. It is a mixture of nationalities from all over the world, particularly so in the last twenty years. It is a multi-cultural patchwork. Certainly there are the normal ties to us through the Crown, but the question of whether Canada will be prepared to take large numbers of our people is going to be a difficult one, to say the least."

Stanton glanced at his notes before continuing. "On the other hand, the Canadians have an excellent record for taking refugees from all over the world. Of more than 3.5 million immigrants admitted to Canada since the end of the Second World War, about 10 per cent came as refugees. They took 37,000 Hungarian refugees in the 1957 period. Between mid-September 1968 to January 10, 1969, they took 9,149 Czech refugees when Czechoslovakia was occupied by the Warsaw Pact armies. In May of 1962 they took one hundred Chinese refugee families from Hong Kong; in 1971, 240 Tibetan refugees; and in 1972, 4,700 Asians expelled from Uganda. We know something about that in this room."

Stanton looked around the room. He foresaw the objection about to be raised and spoke quickly. "I know that the situation here may not qualify our people as refugees, but certainly the same sort of argument can be made, the same sort of sympathies evoked, the same kind of rationale used to convince the Canadians they they should let our people in.

"And I also know that we can expect one hell of a row in Canada when we ask them for an open-gate immigration policy. There is every possibility they may turn us down. You know, they've got a French-Canadian Prime Minister and Quebec is a massive power block in Ottawa."

Agnes Potter asked, "But surely you don't think the Canadians would refuse us. They have such a vast country; they could take millions more people. The size of the country, well, it's enormous. They've got land and resources to spare. Surely. . . . " Her voice trailed off.

An almost imperceptible buzz rose from the telephone in front of the Prime Minister – his was the only one in the room. He picked up the receiver. It was his secretary informing him that the Prime Minister of Canada was on the line. "Good. I'll take it in the Cabinet Secretary's office in just a moment."

He stood, saying to Stanton, "Carry on, Peter. The Canadian Prime Minister is on the line. I shouldn't be too long."

As he left the room, Sands could hear Stanton saying, "Now, as to the United States, they have numerical limitations, 120,000 from the western hemisphere and 170,000 from all other parts of the world, which includes us, and not more than 20,000 visa numbers are available for natives of any single foreign state . . . "

The Prime Minister cut himself off from Stanton's voice as he shut the door of the Secretary's office behind him and went to the telephone. He was alone in the room. Sands knew Roussel well, having attended several Commonwealth conferences at which he had been present. Also he had visited him on three different trips to Canada and the United States. Sands had a high regard for Roussel, a brilliant politician, highly educated, a literate, totally bilingual man with a legal, academic background. Roussel had been left a sizeable fortune by his father, with the result that he had been able to devote his life to teaching, writing, and politics. He carried with him a very strong aura of socialism, a strong nationalistic feeling about his home province of Quebec, and an equally strong desire to preserve the French language and culture. But with regard to the rest of Canada, he was an avowed non-nationalist, a rather paradoxical situation in Sands' view.

Roussel had just left a long meeting with the Kuwaiti ruler and his ministers. The meeting had been a success – the Kuwaitis had agreed to acquire up to two billion dollars in bonds to be issued by PetroCanada, the national oil company which had been established by the government of Canada in 1975.

In turn, PetroCanada would use the funds to support the construction of the Mackenzie valley gas pipeline which was already under construction. It would bring desperately needed natural gas from the Mackenzie delta into Canada south and from the American petroleum fields in Alaska to markets in the mid-western United States and the industrial heart of America, from Chicago east to New York City. The PetroCanada bonds would, of course, be guaranteed by the government of Canada, a condition that the cautious Kuwaitis insisted upon prior to their commitment. In addition, Roussel had been successful in securing an agreement in principle from the Kuwaitis that they would be open to a further debt investment in Canada, government-guaranteed, of up to ten billion dollars over the next five years.

As they opened their conversation, it was obvious to Sands that Roussel was elated by the successful meeting, although he was also extremely concerned about the impact of the Arab action against the United Kingdom. Like Sands, he appreciated that the Kuwaitis were quite able to distinguish between the U.K. on one hand, and Canada on the other. The Arab anger against Great Britain over the clandestine sale of the Rapier missiles to Israel did not rub off on Canada. In fact, the abrupt decision to withdraw all investment funds from the U.K. and to cease all investment there had put the Kuwaitis in a position that day of having to find alternative investment opportunities. Canada, not a new market for the Kuwaitis but one they had largely ignored up until this time, was now of enormous interest to them, particularly since the Prime Minister of Canada had agreed that all withholding taxes normally associated with dividends or interest paid out to foreigners would be waived for all Kuwaiti investments. So that morning, the United Kingdom's loss had become, in part, Canada's gain.

Roussel expressed his deep concern about the plight of Great Britain and of Sands' government. Sands described some of the drastic actions taken by his Cabinet that morning, measures that even the socialist-minded Roussel found to be exceedingly harsh.

When he said so, Sands responded by saying, "Well, Joe, you might think what we've done is drastic. No doubt about it, but there's more to come. We're strapped, we're bankrupt, and if you get right down to it, if we don't take drastic measures, we may well find a revolution on our hands, anarchy and perhaps an overthrow of government. The communist threat in this country is strong. We know that much of the strike activity that has been going on is not only communist-inspired, but communist-led. Those people would like nothing better than to take over the government of this

66

country and run it in dictatorial rather than democratic fashion. The ingredients for a total collapse, not only of the economy but of the government structure – law and order – are present. We must move quickly and decisively, even if some of the moves we have made have been or might be the wrong ones."

"My God, Jeremy. I had no idea things had gone that far," Roussel exclaimed.

"They have, indeed. Now, Joe, the reason for my call is to inform you of the state of things and to ask your government to consider giving the U.K. as much immediate financial support as you can. I must also ask that as to foodstuffs and other basic commodities we've traditionally bought from Canada – wheat, meat, vegetables, and other basic commodities – your government would guarantee payment for all the goods in transit to this country, so that none of it would be diverted or turned back for fear of non-payment."

Roussel's response was immediate. "I have no idea how much we're talking about in terms of money or quantities. I haven't a clue, but I can tell you, Jeremy, that your request is one which the government of Canada will accept. I think that our people should meet immediately to work out emergency arrangements."

"So do I. In fact, I'd like to come and talk with you myself. The Cabinet wants me to go to Washington to meet with the President. It's obvious we need all the financial support we can get from the United States. I need the same food support from the States that I just asked you for. And I need money. In order to get funds, I need the President's support and yours as well, and I need it immediately. Is there any possibility you might stop in London on your way back to Canada, Joe? I leave for the States at seven in the morning and perhaps I could see you before I leave."

"The answer to that one is no, I can't stop over. I leave

67

Kuwait within the hour. I have a Canadian Armed Forces 707 standing by. We'll go direct to the Canadian Forces Base in Lahr, Germany, refuel, and then go straight into Ottawa. My problem is that I am due in Vancouver tomorrow night for a hundred-dollar-a-plate fund-raising dinner. They've sold 2,000 tickets, and I'm the star attraction, at least that's what they tell me. So I've got to be there, there's no choice."

"What time will you be in Vancouver?"

"Just a moment, let me check."

Sands could hear Roussel talking to one of his people. As he waited, Sands sat down heavily, telephone receiver between his left shoulder and ear. He pulled out his pipe, which was still partly filled, lit it, and puffed impatiently on it until Roussel returned.

"I'm due in Vancouver sometime in the morning. I'll be at the Hotel Vancouver. The reception begins at seven, with dinner at eight. I could see you sometime between one and five."

"That's excellent!" exclaimed Sands. "I'll be there as close to one as I can. What I'll do is go direct to see you in Vancouver, then double back to Washington. I think an hour should be more than enough. I know you'll have a heavy schedule while you're in Vancouver, so I'll try to keep it short."

"You'll want to talk about food and money?" Roussel confirmed.

"Yes, and people."

"What do you mean, people."

"My people problem is very simple, Joe. We're faced with a mass exodus from these Islands. Our estimates indicate that about two million people will want to go to Canada. You've probably heard from your High Commissioner here in London of the great queues he's confronted with."

Roussel was aghast. "Two million people? To Canada?

That's almost 10 per cent of our population right now! And Quebec! What about Quebec?"

Sands responded quickly. "I know, Joe. The problems are absolutely horrendous, that's why I just can't deal with you by telephone. I must see you to explain our position."

"God, I knew the U.K. was in bad shape, has been for years and that there might be a collapse, but the people problem, an exodus, as you put it, just never occurred to me. What about the United States, and Australia and New Zealand?"

"We're making the same request to them. That's another reason I am going to see the President. I've got to convince him, as I've got to convince you, to accept an open-gate immigration policy, to change the immigration laws and regulations to allow people to come to North America, those who want to."

Roussel asked, knowing he would have to provide the answers himself, "But where will we put these people? Where would they go? How would they fit into our society? What about jobs for them? And above all, what will they do to the balance between French Canada and the rest of Canada? This is a decision for the Cabinet, and perhaps even for Parliament."

Sands decided to go a step further. "What do you think you would do personally on this question, Joe?"

The reply was slow in coming. "I'd rather not say. There are so many questions to be asked and answered and so many emotional issues . . . no, I . . . I just can't say at this moment. All I can say is I'll get on to my office in Ottawa immediately and get my staff and the appropriate ministries to work to figure out what would happen if we took two million people within a year and whether we could do it, whether we could take part of that number, whether we could take any at all. By the time I see you tomorrow, I should have a much better idea of what we could do. Although I can tell

69

you now that even if investigation showed that we could take all of them, there is no way I can predict what the Cabinet would do. On this issue, I am going to let the Cabinet decide, and I will abide by its decision. Only one thing is certain at this moment, and that is that your disaster is obviously going to be shared by us whether we like it or not."

Roussel was anxious to conclude the conversation. "Jeremy, I've got to get going. It's a long way from Kuwait to Vancouver and there's a lot to be done in between. I'll see you tomorrow."

12:03 PM
Trafalgar Square
London, England

As the Prime Minister concluded his conversation with Roussel, a sequence of events was beginning not a thousand yards away which would demonstrate the proximity of Great Britain to the abyss of anarchy.

It was 12:03 PM as Major Tony Andrews' dark green, box-like armoured personnel carrier (APC) rolled on its clattering tracks along The Mall, then through Admiralty Arch toward Trafalgar Square. Behind him were five more armoured personnel vehicles. Each of the six carried ten men equipped with Makralon Shields, rubber-bullet-firing 1.5″ Federal riot guns, and tear-gas grenades that could be thrown or fired from their guns. They were dressed in battle gear with fragmentation vests and special face-protecting visers in their steel helmets. These troops were specially trained in riot control.

Major Andrews of the Coldstream Guards stood up in the hatchway of his lead vehicle as it passed under Admiralty Arch through the grey drizzle which had continued during the morning. In Trafalgar Square around King Charles' statue and at the foot of Nelson's monument, he could see a crowd of, he guessed, perhaps 10,000 people, which had spilled out onto the pavement. Even at the height of the day there were

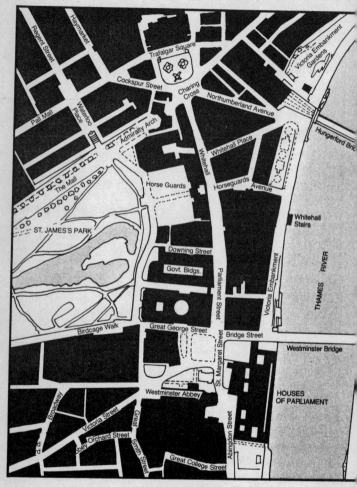

WESTMINSTER

few automobiles and lorries to be seen. The lack of traffic struck Andrews as peculiar until he remembered that this was the day of economic collapse, that everything was stopping, running down, including movement of motor vehicles. As his vehicle entered Charing Cross, Andrews directed the driver to move toward the entrance to Whitehall. The major's orders were to seal off Whitehall and Admiralty Arch, thus containing the mob in Trafalgar Square, should it attempt to move to Downing Street and the government offices. Two of his APCs remained behind to close off the arch.

At the foot of Nelson's monument, but high on a stone ledge so the crowd could easily see her, stood a woman, a loudspeaker in hand. From his distance, Andrews could not see the woman clearly, but as soon as he put his binoculars to his eyes he recognized her. It was Jenny Powis, the militant communist, a professed dedicated revolutionary who entered Parliament in the last election.

When his vehicles were in position, their engines at the idle, Andrews and his men could hear the amplified voice of Jenny Powis, exhorting her listeners to overthrow the government, cursing the Prime Minister and his capitalist, power-hungry followers, enemies of the workers who had brought chaos and disaster to Great Britain and who had personally thrown millions of men and women out of work and taken bread from their mouths. It was time for the working people of England to destroy the ruling classes, to destroy the capitalist government, to destroy the institutions which had oppressed the working people for centuries. They had closed the banks, destroyed the value of our money, and they should be destroyed in turn.

Jenny Powis' voice reached an ear-piercing pitch as she screamed amid an increasing response from the crowd. "Destroy the bastards! Let us march on Downing Street. Let us march on the Parliament Buildings!" The crescendo of

73

noise from the mob mounted to a continuing roar as Jenny Powis leaped down from her perch and, in the vanguard of the herd of hundreds of people, began to move toward Major Andrews' vehicles at the mouth of Whitehall.

Andrews quickly ordered his men out of the personnel carriers and into a line position across the path of the oncoming wave of bodies. His men, nervous, tense, moved quickly into position, some with tear gas grenades in their rifles, others with rubber bullets in their breeches. They pointed their weapons towards the oncoming mass of humanity, many of whom, Andrews saw with dismay, were armed with sticks, clubs, chains, and other weapons, although his trained eye could see no firearms. His sixty men would be no match for this lot, although, he thought hopefully, his commanding officer with another 200 men from his regiment would be in place behind him in a matter of five minutes. But that five minutes might be too late, as, indeed, it was for Major Tony Andrews.

Unarmed, Andrews dismounted from his vehicle, checked to make sure his men were in place and prepared to fire, then moved out across the pavement toward the surging crowd and its resolute leader. When he was about twenty yards out from his carrier, he stopped, raised his right hand above his head, palm out, signalling a halt. Having observed the presence of the troops, the mob had become almost silent as its leading edge approached Andrews' position. When they were a few feet away from him, Powis shouted the order to halt. Jenny Powis, now standing no more than three feet from him, repeated the instruction to the reluctant crowd.

Bringing his right hand down, Andrews yelled at the top of his lungs past Jenny Powis to the crowd, "My orders are that there shall be no access to Whitehall or to The Mall by any person or vehicle. My instructions are that this gathering shall be dispersed if there is any violence or threat of violence."

Then lowering his voice and looking directly into the eyes of Jenny Powis, he said, "I have heard from you threats of violence and I see weapons in the hands of many people in this gathering. I therefore must require that this gathering be dispersed and I ask you, Miss Powis, to co-operate."

In her left hand Jenny Powis held her battery-operated loud speaker, in her right hand a riding crop.

Her response was swift, vicious. "You puppet soldier, you. You and your tin soldiers stand for oppression of the working class. Who do you think you are, telling us what we can and can't do?" With that, her riding crop flashed through the air as she moved to lash out at Andrews. In an instant, he had grabbed her wrist before she could rip the crop across his face.

From that moment, there was total chaos. The crowd erupted with a roar, screaming and shouting, men and women alike surrounded Andrews, beating him relentlessly with their fists, sticks, chains, whatever they had in their hands. Strong as a bull, he fought back, but within a few seconds he was smashed to the ground by a blow at the back of his head. Unconscious, Andrews continued to be beaten, then kicked in the face, groin, anywhere a boot could land on him.

Then the pack turned almost as one to face again the young soldiers, now just a few feet away from them. The taste of blood had brought the mob's emotions to an even higher peak than Jenny Powis had been able to achieve with her passionate words.

They were now ready to destroy those young soldiers facing them, as well as their vehicles and anything that stood in their way.

But a new presence did stand in their way.

While the mob's attention had been focused on the attack on Major Andrews, the rest of his regiment had arrived in their armoured machines, some coming up Whitehall and the rest to The Mall. They had instantly reinforced Andrews' troops, deploying barbed wire coils across portions of the mob's path. The Commanding Officer of the Guards had arrived on the scene in his armoured radio vehicle in time to witness the fate of his young officer.

As the mob gathered itself together for the next advance, the commanding officer did not hesitate. First, he gave the order for gas masks in place. Then at his command the troops opened fire with their rubber bullets at almost point-blank range. At the same time, tear gas grenades were lobbed into the seething mass of humanity gone berserk. The high-intensity wail of the sickening mob-dispersing "Curdler" transmitter ripped across the square.

The front row, which bore the brunt of the rubber bullets, was decimated. People dropped to the pavement screaming, others turned to push, shove, or crawl their way back toward Trafalgar Square as the white clouds of tear gas began to envelop them. The commanding officer ordered his driver to move his armoured radio vehicle into a strategic position in the mouth of the entrance to Whitehall. From that vantage point he could assess the situation. Like Jenny Powis lying unconscious a few yards to the north of him, brought down by a hail of rubber bullets, he too had a battery-powered loud speaker.

He lifted his gas mask from his face and put the loudspeaker to his mouth. Above the screams of pain and panic, the commanding officer's voice boomed across Trafalgar Square, throwing a formal message across this unbelievable scene. "This assembly of people is ordered to disperse forthwith. I say again, this assembly of people is hereby ordered to disperse forthwith. Any person found in Trafalgar Square, or between Trafalgar Square and the entrance to Whitehall or Northumberland, or at the Admiralty Arch after ten minutes will be taken into custody."

Even as he spoke, the Commanding Officer of the Guards

could see that the rubber bullets and tear gas were doing their work. People were streaming through the streets leading to the west, north, and northeast, away from Trafalgar Square, hands and handkerchiefs pressed to their eyes, stumbling as they fled. He looked anxiously for any regrouping or counter-attack by the mob but could see none. The gas lay so thick and heavy over the entire area that he had difficulty in seeing through it. As it began to billow close to him, the commanding officer barked into his radio microphone, which was moni-tored at headquarters. "Raise all the ambulances that can be found!" Then he shouted at a young officer standing next to the radio vehicle: "Price, get out there to Major Andrews!"

Price made no reply, immediately running the few yards to the prostrate form of Major Andrews.

It seemed a very short time until the commanding officer could hear the hooting of sirens as a horde of ambulances descended on Trafalgar Square, picking their way through crowds fleeing the area. After the eighth minute of the commanding officer's edict period, most of the gas had been lifted out of the area by a slight breeze. The only people to be seen in Trafalgar Square were the wounded, felled by the fire of the guardsmen, and others overcome by the tear gas. He estimated that perhaps a hundred people lay scattered around the paved area to the south of Trafalgar Square, where at least twenty ambulances could be seen, their rotating roof lights flashing angrily in the grey drizzle as their crews tended to the casualties.

There were no dead, save one – Major Anthony Andrews of the Coldstream Guards, whose body lay covered with a white sheet in Trafalgar Square, amid the feverish efforts to tend the injuries of those who had struck him down.

12:17 PM
The Cabinet Room
10 Downing Street
London, England

After his telephone discussion with the Prime Minister of Canada, Sands returned to the Cabinet meeting, which he intended to close for luncheon within a few moments. His Foreign Secretary, Peter Stanton, had finished briefing his colleagues on the status of American immigration legislation, quotas, and ceilings, and on the state of the American economy and the unemployment in that nation. Almost everyone in the Cabinet was aware of American economic difficulties, although it was apparent the U.S. was moving out of its recession.

The discussion had turned to whether there should be any incentives for people to leave the U.K. in the form of bonuses or tax exemptions, or whether such inducements would be needed.

The Prime Minister soon became impatient with this subject. "It seems to me that you're discussing only the details of how we implement the open-gate emigration policy. I would prefer to leave that to the Home Secretary and the Foreign Secretary and their staffs to work out. It's obvious to me there will have to be incentives and subsidies; even per-person payments to the governments of the host countries."

He looked at both Secretaries, who silently nodded in agreement.

The Prime Minister continued. "I would be obliged if over lunch all of you would consider whether Parliament should be recalled. Frankly, I think it should. We're involving ourselves in many decisions that really require its approval."

"That's true, Prime Minister. But events have been happening with such speed that decisions must be taken immediately. These are things that have to be done by the Cabinet. There isn't time to call Parliament. There isn't time to debate these minute-to-minute decisions." It was Sir Benjamin Wicks, the Home Secretary, normally an articulate, aggressive man, who had been peculiarly quiet during the Cabinet discussion ever since he had raised the question of attacking and occupying the Arab oil-producing countries. He was a man of enormous wealth, with vast shareholdings in many U.K. manufacturing corporations, all of which he had had to put into a blind trust before he accepted the Prime Minister's offer of a ministry. He had earned his money the hard way in spite of handicaps of class and an almost impossible taxation climate. Sands speculated that Wicks had been preoccupied this morning not only by being shot down on his invasion proposal, but as well by the spectre of the real possibility that he would lose everything, as would countless other Britons on this crisis day.

However, for whatever reason, Wicks had decided to take part in the session. Sands was pleased to have his viewpoint. Wicks had more to say.

"As a matter of fact, I think we're discussing one of the key reasons for the decline of the British Empire and the United Kingdom. In my opinion, the parliamentary system in the form we have it in the United Kingdom is totally obsolete. It evolved over centuries of slow progress, when communications were slow, when there were no instant problems needing instant solutions, when the voting public knew little or nothing about what was going on in the world. This is the day of fast action and quick response. In my view, our creaky old system is just not geared to it. So far as I am concerned, Prime Minister, in a crisis, it should be up to the Cabinet in consultation with the leaders of the other parties – and there are only two of them in this country, thank God – to make all the decisions. The government can report to Parliament, get the advice of Parliament, take its lumps if you will, when the crisis has passed.

"But if we accept the proposition that the things we've been doing must be ratified by Parliament before we can act on them in an emergency crisis of this kind, well, it's ridiculous, Prime Minister. Someday there may be a new mechanism, but not today."

The Prime Minister lit his pipe once again as he listened to Wicks.

"Quite right, Benjamin, quite right. We may be closer to a change in the system of government than you think. The real question in my mind is whether it's going to be a democratic form based on free elections, or whether it's going to be a communist dictatorship type. I can smell anarchy."

As the Prime Minister spoke, the first sounds of the Trafalgar Square mob were heard through the closed windows of the Cabinet Room, which face north overlooking the Horse Guards Parade, the large paved square where the annual ceremony of the Trooping of the Colour takes place. To the north of it lies Admiralty Arch, the entrance to Charing Cross and Trafalgar Square.

When the first mighty roar was heard Agnes Potter exclaimed, "Good heavens, what's that?!" The same question was in the minds of everyone in the Cabinet Room except the Defence Secretary, Lord Cutting.

"In the last hour," he said, "my staff have kept me

informed of a mass rally in Trafalgar Square, organized by communist labour leaders and Communist Party members to protest the closing of the banks, the loss of jobs, the apparent collapse of the economy and, of course, this wretched government."

"It hasn't taken them very long to get a rally organized," Stanton commented dryly.

"It never does, Peter," Lord Cutting responded. "It never does."

The sounds of another roar reached them.

"How many people are in this rally, John," the Prime Minister asked, "and what's being done about it?"

"About ten thousand people," Cutting replied. "There's a large number of police there, but of course they're unarmed. I've authorized the guards – they've had extensive experience in Northern Ireland – to move in their armoured personnel carriers to seal off Whitehall and The Mall to prevent any movement of the mob toward the government offices and the Parliament Buildings."

Again Agnes Potter interjected. "But you don't really think that an assembly of British people, of Englishmen in Trafalgar Square, is going to riot or take the law into its own hands, do you? Surely!"

"My dear lady, there is absolutely no doubt about it in my mind whatsoever. Our intelligence people have informed me that the organizers and leaders of the rally are militant activists totally dedicated to violence and the overthrow of the government of the United Kingdom. This is the moment they've been waiting for. This is the hour they've been working for since the end of the war."

As he spoke, the sound of another roar filled the room, followed this time by the clatter of gunfire. Several members of the Cabinet involuntarily leaped up, shocked. "My God, they're shooting!" someone exclaimed.

The Prime Minister spoke sternly. "Please, please, do sit down. There's no need to panic. We must be calm. We must get on with the running of this country. I'm certain our military are totally loyal, and I'm also certain they're perfectly capable of handling whatever is going on in Trafalgar Square." Seats were resumed, although some ministers obeyed grudgingly, others with embarrassed looks on their faces.

Sands turned again toward the Defence Secretary. "Lord Cutting, I would be obliged if you would keep the Cabinet informed of any information you receive from your staff concerning the events taking place in Trafalgar Square at this moment, or any other comparable situations which might be occurring elsewhere. And I would also be obliged if you and your staff should consider the question of whether martial law ought to be declared throughout the whole of the United Kingdom; and if so, what steps should be taken not only to declare martial law, but to enforce it as well."

1:03 PM
The Kuwait Hilton
Kuwait

Joseph Roussel put down the telephone receiver. He was badly shaken by the conversation he had just had with Jeremy Sands about the crisis in the U.K. brought about by, among others, his Arab hosts the Kuwaitis, in concert with Saudi Arabia and the other Arab OPEC nations. The mind of the Prime Minister of Canada raced as he sought to sort out the implications for his own country. What would happen to the deal he had just arranged with the Kuwaitis? They had known of the action against the U.K. but had said nothing about it that morning in their discussions.

What would the economic ramifications be for Canada, which had a large trading surplus, particularly in raw materials shipped to Great Britain? What financial aid, if any, could Canada afford to give?

But for Roussel the mind-boggling question was this: how could Canada accept two million immigrants in twelve months? An open-gate immigration policy? Almost inconceivable. Where would these people go in Canada? Where would they live? What would the effect be on the economy, the work force? And above all, what would the effect be on Quebec? What would this do to Confederation? After the many political scandals in Quebec in 1975, the cause of the separatists and the Parti Québecois, the political party advocating separation, had advanced rapidly, although they had not yet come to power.

Roussel had agreed to meet with the British Prime Minister the next afternoon in Vancouver. There was no time to be lost.

"Pierre!" he shouted for the Principal Secretary of the Prime Minister's Office, Pierre Pratte, who had accompanied him and André Vachon, the Canadian Minister of Finance. Pratte appeared in the doorway of the sitting room of the luxurious suite. He was Roussel's longtime friend, faithful ally, staunch supporter, confidant, and adviser.

"*Oui,* Joe?" Pratte always addressed the Prime Minister informally and in French when they were in private or among close acquaintances, but always with precise formality when in the presence of others.

"We've got a disaster on our hands. Get your notebook so I can dictate some instructions and ask André to join us, please."

"What's wrong?"

"The Arabs have pulled out on the United Kingdom. The Brits have an economic crisis on their hands."

When he had returned with the Finance Minister, Pratte was ready to take notes. Roussel went over the details of his conversation with Sands, raising exclamations of shock and surprise from his listeners as he recounted the discussion.

"I've agreed to meet Sands in Vancouver tomorrow afternoon. He insists on seeing me face to face. He's got money problems. He's got food problems and he wants to talk about an open-gate immigration policy. He'll meet me at the hotel around two, then he'll double back to Washington to meet with the President. The Chancellor of the Exchequer is on his way across to Washington now."

"I wonder where the Secretary of State is at this moment?" Vachon interjected.

"I'm not sure, but something tells me she's in Moscow," Roussel speculated. "Strangely enough, I think she's there to have preliminary discussions with the Soviets on the possibility of a Middle East Arms Limitations agreement. Meanwhile the Arabs, by bringing down the axe on the neck of Great Britain, are implementing their own form of MEAL. Anyway, where she is is the President's problem, not mine."

Roussel, in shirt sleeves in the air-conditioned suite, stood up, walked over to the amply supplied bar, and poured himself a stiff shot of rye. Pratte cringed inwardly. When Joe started at this time of the day, he usually wound up going for twenty-four hours, then collapsing in bed somewhere, out of his mind. One could only hope for the best.

The Prime Minister, glass in hand, went to the closed glass door leading to the balcony. He looked out across the heat-shimmering flat of the desert, northward to the huge tank farms spread along the coastline of this fabulously rich sheikdom. About a mile offshore, moored to the pipeline-carrying docks, he could see the long, squat hulls of a series of supertankers taking on their precious cargos of costly crude oil. Further offshore, sitting anchored motionless in the calm grey sea, sat another four vessels, empty, riding high out of the water, their reddish-orange bottoms contrasting with the drab grey and black colours of their hulls. Inland to the northeast, just beyond the horizon, could be seen the ever-present black smoke from the natural gas being flared off, burned, and wasted, at the heads of hundreds of crude-oil production wells. From the time of his arrival in Kuwait and his first sight of the natural gas being flared off, Roussel had been appalled at the waste of this commodity in such critically short supply in the United States. He could not understand why liquefaction plants and liquid natural gas tankers were not being built in abundance to capture the gas and ship it to North America.

He shrugged, shut out the fascinating sight outside, and turned his mind back to the crisis Sands had dropped in his lap. That was it. It had been literally dropped in his lap. No fault of his. No control over the situation. Leave it to the English.

His drink was already half gone.

"What time will that aircraft be ready to go?" he asked Pratte.

"Whenever you are."

"Okay. We'll leave here in about fifteen minutes." He remained standing, his back to the window, glass in hand. His mind functioned faster now, as he felt the first effects of the good booze.

He started to think out loud. "It seems to me our major short-term problem is not the loss of trade with the U.K., assuming the collapse is as severe as Sands says it is. And it won't be the lending of two or three billion – he'll probably want a lot more. We can also look after getting food to them, wheat, meat, butter, vegetables, all that stuff. Canada's real problem will be this business of immigration. What does he call it? I told you, Pierre . . ."

"The open-gate immigration policy."

"Yes, yes, open-gate immigration policy. And he said 10 per cent, about six million people in a year, have to get off the Islands, and maybe two million, perhaps even more, wanting to come to Canada. Okay, so the question breaks into two parts. First, what position will Quebec take, and what will my own Cabinet do? Will Quebec feel strongly enough about this to threaten to secede? I don't know." He paused and walked over to the bar.

Vachon quietly suggested, "But isn't the real question, Joe, what you, what the Cabinet is going to do?"

Roussel was back at the window again, a fresh drink in his hand. "Sure, but it's Quebec which will be the key to the Cabinet decision."

"Are you saying that if Quebec says, 'No, you can't take them,' that means the federal government will automatically say no?"

Roussel snapped back. "Of course not."

"But if Quebec says they're against it and they threaten to secede, what then?" Pratte asked.

The Prime Minister shrugged. "Who knows? But the question of whether Canada will take any of *les anglais* or none at all, that is the first question. So what I want is a telegram, a message, you know how to do it, Pierre, to each of the premiers of the provinces. It should go something like this – you can fix it up."

Roussel's message was dictated in hesitating fashion, interspersed with sips of rye and soda, then edited and telephoned by Pratte to his own secretary at her home in Ottawa (it was just 6:15 AM there). It read:

As you know, the United Kingdom is in an economic collapse. I have been informed by the Prime Minister of Great Britain that his government considers it absolutely mandatory that provision be made for the emigration of approximately 10 per cent of the population of the U.K. Islands within the next twelve months because of food and employment shortages, with this exodus beginning immediately. The U.K. government estimates two million people will want to go to Canada. The U.K. has adopted an open-gate emigration policy and will subsidize all travel. The advice of your government as to whether Canada should adopt a reciprocal open-gate immigration policy is imperative. Also supply the advice of your government as to how a large number of people could be temporarily housed and accommodated in your province for the next two or three years should my government's decision be in the affirmative. Prime Minister Sands will meet with me in Vancouver tomorrow afternoon. I will not give him an answer at that time, but will listen to the reasons why the open-gate policy should be adopted and why it is critical that it be implemented immediately. The federal Cabinet will meet on Wednesday, July 7 at 8:00 PM to resolve this question and to consider what financial and food-supply assistance can be given to the U.K. Your advice on these matters should have been communicated to me before that time.

Pratte also instructed his secretary to send a copy of the telegram to each federal Cabinet minister with instructions that it was imperative that each and every one of them attend the scheduled Cabinet meeting Wednesday night, and that certain ministers would be instructed to have their staffs produce crash programs of research and opinion on the impact of the potential mass immigration. He asked that the following ministers be asked to alert their staffs to expect questions: Urban Affairs, Transport, Labour, Manpower and Immigration, and the Secretary of State in connection with bilingualism and bicultural problems. A special set of questions on food supply was sent to the Minister of Agriculture. Vachon would instruct his own staff later concerning the extent to which Canada could go on a loan to the U.K.

While Pratte telephoned to Ottawa, Roussel and Vachon prepared the immigration questions. Roussel took a sip of his drink, then got a grip on himself, went into the bathroom, and poured it down the sink. As he returned to the room, he announced to Vachon with a smile, "I'll have the second drink on the aircraft."

The last of the immigration questions was written down just as Pratte re-emerged from his Ottawa conversation.

Assuming that within twelve months Canada will admit two million Britons:

1) Where would they go in Canada
   a) if directed?
   b) if not directed?

2) Can accommodation be found?
   a) What temporary housing facilities exist in what locations, e.g., old Armed Forces Bases, or abandoned mining or other communities?
   b) How much rental accommodation or vacant space including habitable factories is available in all urban communities (outside Quebec), e.g., trailers, mobile homes, and trailer/camping parks?

3) If immigrants are directed to specific locations, what means would be used for control, policing, work permits, employment?

4) How many will be black or from India or Pakistan, or should Canada accept only native-born Britons?

5) What will the reaction of Quebec be?

6) What new job opportunities exist and where?

7) What will the reaction of labour unions be?

8) How will funding of immigrants take place while they work themselves into the economy? How much per person or per family?

9) Could new towns be built quickly? What industries could be set up in temporary new towns?

89

10) Could land grants be made of arable sections of the mid-Canada region?

11) What are the costs of a mass move? Estimate all air facilities plus ships available, and the number of people that could be handled each month.

12) What would be the main points of disembarkation by ship? What rail facilities are available to transport immigrants to their destination?

13) What kind of lead time will be necessary to create the reception mechanism? (Minister of Manpower and Immigration to be responsible for organization and co-ordination.)

By the time Pratte finished sending these questions to Ottawa, not just fifteen minutes had passed, as the Prime Minister had predicted, but almost an hour. By 2:35 PM local time, when the Canadian Armed Forces white Boeing 707 lifted off from the Kuwait airport, the Prime Minister of Canada was well into his third drink.

Prime Minister Joseph Roussel was still sleeping it off when the engines of the Boeing 707 shut down at Canadian Forces Base, Lahr, Germany, to refuel and take on a full load of military personnel, some with dependants, all bound for Canada. On departing Kuwait, the flight attendant had laid out the Prime Minister's bed in the private compartment at the front of the 707. Roussel had collapsed on it in fatigue and alcohol-induced oblivion three hours earlier.

"Joe." Pierre Pratte lightly shook his left shoulder. "Joe, wake up. We've landed at Lahr."

Pratte watched as Roussel flopped over on his back, face flushed, red and puffy eyes opening slowly to attempt to focus on him. The alcohol was still there, but Pierre Pratte knew that this hard-drinking man could pull himself together fairly rapidly and carry on in such a way that a stranger would not detect that he was still carrying a reasonable amount of alcohol in his body. But those who knew him well could tell; first among those being his wife of thirty-six years, Manon. He had found her when helping a friend – he'd even forgotten his name – who was running for office in Val d'Or. She was petite, charming, vivacious, pretty, the eighteen-year-old daughter of a local *boulanger*. Sexy, ripe, loveable. After raising six chil-

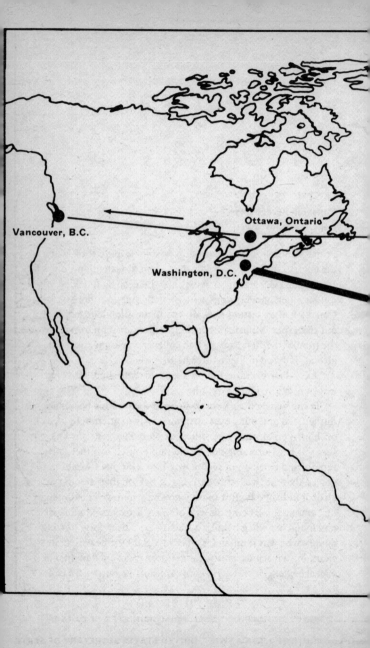

Vancouver, B.C.

Ottawa, Ontario

Washington, D.C.

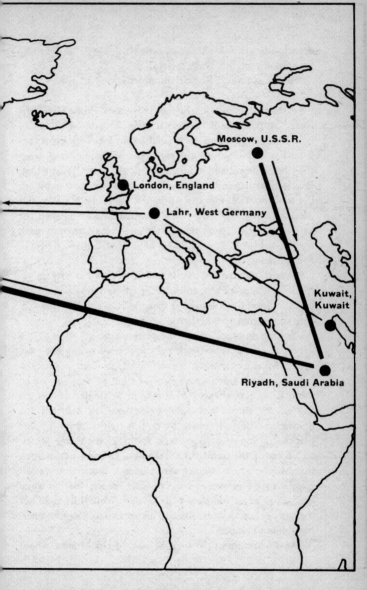

Moscow, U.S.S.R.

London, England

Lahr, West Germany

Kuwait, Kuwait

Riyadh, Saudi Arabia

———— ROUTE OF JOSEPH ROUSSEL, PRIME MINISTER OF CANADA

━━━ ROUTE OF JESSICA SWIFT, UNITED STATES SECRETARY OF STATE

dren to maturity, Manon had become a dowdy and dumpy grandmother figure. Plain, fat, sexless.

"We're at Lahr?" Roussel mumbled.

"*Oui.*"

A startled, almost fearful look crossed the Prime Minister's face. "Manon, she'll be here waiting for me!" Reeking of liquor, he struggled to get up and on his feet with assistance from Pratte. He moved quickly to the washroom, staggering slightly. As he entered it, he shouted, "My razor!" Pratte took the electric razor out of Roussel's bag and handed it to him in the washroom. Within three minutes, the Prime Minister had used the razor, washed his face, combed his hair, cleaned out his mouth with a harsh mouthwash he always carried to mask the alcohol smell, slipped on his suitcoat, straightened his tie, and was ready.

"What's the name of the Base Commander here, Pierre?"

"John Clifford, Colonel John Clifford. And the Commander of Canadian Forces Europe is General Howard, Bill Howard. You've met him several times."

Roussel nodded. "He should be here also."

He was. Just as the front passenger door swung open the Prime Minister spotted Howard's round face under the heavily gold-braided green general's hat at the foot of the ramp. Roussel could also see Manon in the small crowd at the foot of the steps, her round figure sporting a bright red lightweight dress, topped by a flowered helmet-like hat perched on top of her grey hair. Although the Prime Minister's focus on the scene was not the best, he quickly calculated that Manon's new clothes were evidence that his American Express card has been given a full-scale French workout while she was in Paris and he was in Kuwait. Well, if it made her look any better. . . . He focused his eyes more sharply on her. No, it hadn't helped.

At the bottom of the steps he bent to kiss Manon, whose

smile disappeared instantly when she caught the sharp smell of alcohol. After a few words with her, he turned to the green-uniformed officers who had turned out en mass, at least so it appeared to him, to greet him. Both the Commander of CFE and the Base Commander were flattered when he called them by name.

Roussel barely saw the faces of the officers and their wives as he shook their hands. His mind was gearing up and away from the effects of the liquor. Inwardly he was examining some of the major problems he had to deal with, while outwardly he was exchanging pleasantries with these good Canadian military men and their ladies.

He felt the touch of a hand on his left elbow from behind. It was a familiar gesture, a signal that Pierre Pratte wanted his attention. Without looking behind or taking his eyes off the people he was talking with, he canted his head slightly to the left.

Pratte whispered. "Gaston wants to talk with you urgently. He's on the line on the telephone in the terminal manager's office." Gaston Belisle, the Premier of Quebec. There would be no doubt about why he wanted to talk.

The Prime Minister smiled apologetically to the officers. "Excuse me please. I have a most urgent telephone call." Turning, he took Manon by the arm. Then, flanked by the Base Commander and the Commander of CFE and their wives, and followed by André Vachon and Pierre Pratte, he walked directly to the terminal building, a dingy, ancient, German hangar, which now was used by the Air Transport Group of the Canadian forces as its Lahr passenger terminal. Roussel knew exactly where he was going. He led the way through the entrance doors, then to the VIP room on the right, where he left Manon in the care of Vachon and Pratte. Then the Prime Minister went directly to the terminal manager's office. The manager handed him the telephone and left the room, closing the door behind him.

"Hello, Gaston."

"One moment sir. I will get him on the line for you." It was Belisle's secretary. Roussel felt the twinge of anger he always felt when he was left waiting by people who, thinking they are busy or superior, instruct their secretaries to get Mr. So-and-So on the line, then require Mr. So-and-So to wait until the caller himself deigns to put in an appearance. Finally Belisle came on the line.

"Joe? Are you there?"

"Yes, yes, Gaston. I'm here. What can I do for you?" These two men knew each other. They were close, of the same political party. Their families were intermarried. Elite, wealthy, well educated, they had always moved in the same social circles. They had the same cultural and language goals for Quebec and all of French Canada. Both men were non-nationalists when it came to Canada, and avowedly so, whereas both were gut nationalists about *la belle province* of Quebec, a sort of French-language Texas in central Canada.

Even so, Joseph Roussel was a federalist. He knew the real source of power was in the federal government in Ottawa. And since the power was there, so was Joseph Roussel. He and his handful of colleagues went to Ottawa when they decided to join the party of which he was now the leader. As a federalist, Roussel was dedicated to the proposition of keeping Canada together, pacifying Quebec to ensure that it would stay within the Confederation, and mollifying the strong, separatist trends which had developed in British Columbia and oil- and gas-rich Alberta. Alberta lay astride the vast, sedimentary belt in the central west and north, with its enormous deposits of crude oil and natural gas, and the potentially highly productive tar sands deposits. For decades, but more particularly in the past six years, the two western provinces had grown more and more alienated from what they called the "east" or "central Canada," and, more particularly, from the bureaucracy of Ottawa where decisions were made, they claimed, by faceless "mandarins" who had no knowledge of or interest in the problems of western Canada. There were continuing complaints about freight rates, about Ontario and Quebec ripping off the energy resources of the west, and a host of other injustices. The anti-east pro-separatist movement had grown by leaps and bounds in the far west from the time when the federal government had unilaterally imposed an export tax on crude oil to keep Canadian prices in line with the OPEC countries. By doing that, Ottawa had insured that the windfall profits from the massive jumps in those prices went to the federal government and not to the province of Alberta or the producers. The fact that the tax impost would be used to subsidize the cost of OPEC crude oil which had to be brought into Quebec and the Maritimes at world prices drew little sympathy from the west.

But nowhere was the idea of separation so strong as it was in Quebec, where *les anglais* were, if not detested, disliked with increasing animosity. To the *Québecois* anyone in the rest of Canada who spoke English was English-Canadian, whether he was German, Italian, Pakistani, or whatever. The fact that the percentage of people of British descent in the rest of Canada was now quite small had nothing to do with it. The French-Canadians, while fighting to preserve their language and culture, had become militant against anything "English."

The government of the province of Quebec had renamed its legislative assembly the National Assembly. Language bills had been passed making French the official language in the province. Every effort was being made to make it difficult for a child to be educated in the English language. Quebec government contracts discriminated against bidders from outside Quebec. And only recently, while on a cheek-kissing

97

state visit to France, the Premier himself had disclosed his intent to move toward separation and independence. He had been quoted as saying, "I find that we can have a French Quebec in North America within a Canadian Common Market with an original idea of sovereignty without plunging the population of Quebec into an adventure." The move toward separation was growing.

If the sudden influx into the rest of Canada – they would never go into Quebec – of two million English-speaking Britons within a year was added to the already explosive situation in Quebec, what then? Would Quebec fight such a decision? In the mind of the Prime Minister of Canada, Joseph Roussel, there was absolutely no doubt whatsoever.

He said, "I guess you want to talk about the open-gate immigration policy question. You must have my telegram by now."

Belisle acknowledged. "Yes, I have your telegram, and yes, I want to talk about the open-gate immigration policy. Such a policy is totally unacceptable to my government. Joseph, how in the name of heaven could you, a son of Quebec, a French-Canadian through and through, how could you possibly support this insane idea? Quebec is your nation, yours and mine. It is inconceivable that you would even allow this ridiculous suggestion to be considered. If you were *anglais*, if you were from Toronto, or from anywhere outside Quebec for that matter, I could understand it. But, you, Joseph Roussel, how could you do this? I just do not understand."

This was exactly the response Roussel knew he would get from Gaston Belisle, whom he knew so well. But he had not expected it to be so hostile, so personal.

"Now, just a minute, Gaston. I have done nothing more than to communicate to you and the other premiers that this urgent request has been made by the United Kingdom in the face of the economic collapse they're going through. I have not said that I am supporting the proposition of bringing two million English into Canada within a year. No, I have never said such a thing. I am only one man in the country. I cannot and will not make a decision on a question of this magnitude unilaterally. You know better than anyone that I cannot. There is no possible way I could say to the Prime Minister of the United Kingdom, 'I hear your message, but I am French-Canadian. There is no possible way I will let your people in. I will not allow it!' Gaston, I am the Prime Minister of Canada. I am not the Prime Minister of Quebec. Quite apart from any racial and cultural reasons, quite apart from the nationalistic interests of Quebec, Canada must consider the request for humane reasons. You know, Gaston, we're dealing with the lives of people, men, women and children. The question must be considered seriously by the federal government. There is no choice."

Belisle's response was curt. "You do have a choice, Prime Minister, and it is this. Your telegram says you will call a special meeting of your Cabinet at eight o'clock on Wednesday night. I will call a special meeting of the National Assembly of Quebec to begin at two o'clock Wednesday afternoon. I will present a motion to the National Assembly which I'm certain even the opposition will support."

The Prime Minister of Canada, perspiring in the cool, air-conditioned office under the onslaught of the Premier of Quebec and the residue of his drinking, returned the cloak of formality and enmity now put on by his lifelong friend, "And what is this magic resolution, Mr. Premier?"

The response of Gaston Belisle was immediate. "It will be a motion that Quebec should secede from Canada."

Tuesday July 6

6:15 AM
Heathrow Airport
London, England

The Prime Minister had been dozing during the half hour ride from 10 Downing Street to Heathrow Airport, where a VC-10 aircraft of the Queen's Flight was waiting in the continuing drizzle to take him to North America. He was exhausted. He had had less than four hours of sleep and wouldn't have had that except that his wife burst in upon him in his library office shortly after two, insisting that he get some sleep. Sands' wife of forty years, Mary, was a simple, unaffected, country girl from the same town where he was born and raised, Bude in Cornwall. She had always been a force to reckon with. He had given in – there was no choice – and off to bed he had gone, while Mary had "thrown some things in a bag" for him for the fast trip to America.

Mary knew the North American climate well, having visited Ottawa, Vancouver, Washington, and New York during mid-summer. It would be very warm, probably hot. No need to pack any heavy clothes or an overcoat. She had packed for him a hundred times before, knew everything he required. One thing he rarely needed was that she accompany him, which pleased her enormously. Mary really hated to travel. Besides, there were so many things to do in keeping their household at 10 Downing Street, or wherever they were living at the moment, going smoothly.

However, at this moment, Mary Sands was deeply concerned for her husband. The ordinary strain and pressure on him as Prime Minister was bad enough, but the events of the past day by themselves left a mark on him. It seemed to Mary, as she watched her husband pull himself together, get dressed, and leave 10 Downing Street that morning in the early light, that he looked a little more stooped, a little older, a little more preoccupied, and that he moved a little slower than he ever had.

Jeremy Sands was indeed an exhausted man, but he was also a determined, stubborn Englishman, who refused to give up, who had to keep going, who seemed to have an inexhaustible source of energy that would see him through. And he would draw on that limitless energy and on that stubbornness to get his country and himself through this horrendous crisis.

Notwithstanding the decision of Cabinet that he should go to America and Teheran, the Prime Minister was apprehensive about leaving the country at this time of catastrophe. There would be new events, new crises, new decisions that would have to be made while he was away. In his absence, would the Cabinet be able to make the right decisions? Would Stanton, as Acting Prime Minister, provide the necessary leadership?

On the other hand, Stanton could be in touch with him almost instantly, no matter where he was, whether in his car, halfway across the Atlantic, or in Vancouver or Washington. And anyway, he was the only person who could negotiate directly with the President of the United States, the Prime Minister of Canada, and the Shah of Iran over the crucial matters of financial support, a continued supply of life-and-industry-sustaining crude oil, and the mass movement of people out of the United Kingdom.

During Monday afternoon, the Prime Minister had consulted at length with the Leader of the Opposition, Tom Short, to inform him of the decisions the government had made and to obtain his advice on what additional actions should be taken, including an unprecedented declaration of martial law. While the leader, true to form, did not approve all of the steps the Cabinet had taken, he and the Prime Minister were of one mind that before martial law should be declared – a final, unspeakable act in the motherland of parliamentary democracy – there would have to be clear evidence of a widespread revolt of the people. While the Trafalgar riot was unmistakable proof that the seeds of revolution were strong and vigorously nurtured by the Communist Party, that uprising was not in itself sufficient to justify the imposition of martial law. However, the Prime Minister undertook to keep Thomas Short informed of any indication of further uprisings or riots and to consult with him before martial law might be declared. In his temporary absence from the country, Stanton, the Acting Prime Minister, would consult with Short.

The final point of discussion between the two men was on the question of whether a National Government ought to be formed, a bringing together of all parties in the House of Commons during the crisis period, just as had been done in the Second World War. Short had agreed that it might well be in the national interest for a National Government to be formed, provided an appropriate number of places be made available in the Cabinet for him and certain of his senior colleagues. But it was decided that a decision should not be taken until the Prime Minister returned from his emergency trip, which should be Thursday, at the latest. Provided that the government agreed to consult him on all major matters being considered by the Cabinet in the interval, the Leader of the Opposition would not insist on the recall of Parliament until a decision to form or not form a National Government had been taken.

As a matter of courtesy, the Prime Minister also met with the leader of the Liberal Party, going over the same ground he had covered with the Leader of the Opposition, although he made no offer to consult him on all the major issues being considered by the Cabinet. It was agreed that if a National Government was to be formed, the Liberal leader would have a place in the Cabinet.

The Prime Minister had spent the time between the termination of the Cabinet meeting and his wife's order to go to bed, conferring with Cabinet ministers who wanted advice. And he had met at length with the head of the Trades Unions Congress, mainly to ask that the TUC do everything in its power to get its constituent unions to agree not to strike for any reason during the crisis period. It was necessary that productivity in the industrial complex of the nation should be maintained, so that food and essential commodities entered the country without fear of stoppage and that important exports continued to flow.

Over the long haul, the calamitous drop in the value of the pound sterling against the U.S. dollar would serve to stimulate Britain's export trade enormously because the price of its products would be highly competitive. But for the short haul, it was absolutely essential that existing jobs be preserved. The head of the TUC had agreed to do everything he could to comply, but had ruefully pointed out to the Prime Minister that the attempts of the TUC to have its member unions hold the wage line during the days of the ill-fated Social Compact of the mid-seventies had in the end result totally failed.* So the Prime Minister should understand that no guarantees

* As had the government's 1975 wage increase limit of 10 per cent

106

could be made, nor was there any assurance that even if legislation was to be passed there would be compliance by the trade unions.

However, with unemployment now hitting unprecedented levels of over two million and with the limited ability of the government to continue to finance dole payments, there was no doubt there would be a new keenness on the part of workers to maintain and keep their jobs and to abstain from what might under the circumstances be called the "luxury" of striking.

The TUC would fully support the open-gate emigration policy, no doubt about that, and perhaps the mass exodus would take with it some of the principal communists and other troublemaking unionists.

Just before 7:00 PM the Chancellor of the Exchequer, Hobson, had called from Washington to say that the President had asked that the meeting be postponed until the Secretary of State had arrived back from Moscow, which would be at noon tomorrow, Tuesday, possibly even later. There was no alternative but to go along with that request.

Hobson indicated to the Prime Minister that he was unsure who would be with the President at the meeting other than the Secretaries of State and Labor, and possibly Housing. The Prime Minister asked Hobson to deal with the question of direct American financial support, as well as assistance in obtaining International Monetary Fund monies and also monies from the OECD fund. Also, it was critical to get the Americans to help in sorting out both a new source of supply of crude oil for the U.K., as well as the continued financing of its purchase. Sands suggested that perhaps they might agree to approach both the Shah and Venezuela on Britain's behalf. The last thing in the world he wanted to do was to have to attend upon the Shah. In any event, Hobson was also to press for the American acceptance of the open-gate flow of immigrants, although under no circumstances was he to press the point so far as to get a "no." If he detected any indication of a negative attitude, he was to leave the question until the Prime Minister was on the scene. That principle was to apply to any part of the negotiations.

Sands estimated he would be arriving at Washington's Dulles International Airport between ten and eleven the next night, and would be obliged if Hobson would meet him there. Should there be any instructions or advice Hobson required in the course of negotiations, he should feel free to be in touch with Sands at any time. The Secretary of the Cabinet would have details as to how to reach him at any point during his trip to North America.

The Prime Minister had decided to travel alone except for his private secretary, Roger Prentice, who would look after all travel and accommodation details, as well as the papers and documents Sands would need. Sands had thought about making the trip by himself, but decided that with the necessity to go on to Teheran from Washington, he would definitely need Prentice's assistance.

The Defence Secretary had been concerned for the security of the Prime Minister. Cutting had wanted him taken to Heathrow from 10 Downing Street in an armoured personnel carrier, but Sands had rejected the idea. Instead, he and Prentice had taken the huge black Rolls Royce limousine normally assigned to the Prime Minister, a vast, comfortable machine in which the exhausted Prime Minister had promptly fallen asleep as they entered Whitehall from Downing Street for the uneventful journey to Heathrow Airport.

Sands awoke as the Rolls Royce turned off the M4 for the last mile into Heathrow. He glanced at his watch. It was 6:55. A fast trip. Unusual. There were very few cars on the road into this normally bustling major airfield. There were two of the double-decker airport buses ahead and one behind, both with their peculiar baggage trailers, but there were no cars to be seen. "Very strange, Prentice. There's really no traffic at all."

"Yes, I noticed it too, sir. Hard to believe that the country has, I guess you'd have to say, stopped in its tracks."

The two men remained silent as the black motor car passed the international terminal and through a gate which was opened by policemen; then out across the ramp, past the silent 707s, 747s, Lockhead 1011s, Tridents, Comets, and other aircraft with myriad international markings and names on their fuselages and tails. Finally they reached the hulking VC-10, which awaited them with its front passenger door open, steps down and in place, and brightly flashing lights reflecting off the rain-covered fuselage.

As Sands' limousine approached the aircraft, he could see the familiar face of the pilot. Squadron Leader Basil Robins of the Royal Air Force moved quickly down the wet steps to greet him, blue trenchcoat done up at the back to fend off the heavy rain. His blue officer's cap sat squarely and firmly on his head. In his left hand was an opened umbrella for the Prime Minister's protection.

Sands could also see two mechanics fastening the lower cowling of the outboard starboard engine back in place while two other men stood by the energizing cart which would supply the extra electrical power needed to get the engines started. The Prime Minister's car came to a gentle stop. Squadron Leader Robins immediately opened the door to be greeted by the Prime Minister as he got out doing up his trenchcoat. "Good morning, Basil."

Robins gave him a smart palm-out RAF salute, returning the greeting. "Good morning, sir. We're all set to go." He handed the Prime Minister the umbrella.

"If you'll go on board, Prime Minister, I'll give Mr. Prentice

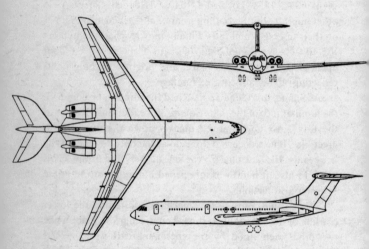

VC-10 FOUR-JET LONG-RANGE TRANSPORT

a hand with the bags. My crewmen are just finishing some slight repairwork as you can see."

Sands took the umbrella. "No, it's all right, Basil. Prentice and the driver can manage between them. Tell me, what's wrong with the engine?"

"We had a bird strike in the final approach as we came in here. We got a good thump on the starboard side when we were about two hundred feet off the deck. Made a dent in the leading edge of the wing. But I wanted the engines checked to make sure we didn't get one of our feathered friends ingested. They can make a mess of an engine."

The Prime Minister moved toward the steps. He was concerned. "You're sure the engines are all right?"

"Certainly, sir."

Within five minutes the steps were raised and the doors secured. Robins had completed startup, assisted by his first officer, Flight Lieutenant Cranston, and Flight Engineer Jason Rupert. This crew was one of the top teams in the RAF. Robins, a superlative, experienced pilot, enjoyed the confidence of the Queen's husband and son, both of whom were pilots. The Prime Minister and various of his colleagues had flown with this man many times. He was among the best.

But like pilots young and old, inexperienced and experienced, there is a time when a value judgement, a calculated risk, is taken in the presence of exceptional circumstances. Squadron Leader Basil Robins would make such a calculated judgement during this important trip. At Heathrow Airport, at 7:17 AM, Tuesday, July 6, the VC-10's final pre-take-off checks were completed. Over the radio, the co-pilot received and copied from Air Traffic Control the clearance for the flight plan and route to Goose Bay, Labrador. There they would deliver a part for a waiting Andover aircraft of the Queen's Flight, refuel, then proceed on to Vancouver. In case of complications, Robins' alternate airport would be Frobisher Bay at the southern end of Baffin Island in the Northwest Territories of Canada. The weather at Goose Bay was already marginal.

Take-off clearance was received. The huge aircraft swung onto the runway centre line, then gathered speed as Robins, assisted by Cranston, eased the throttles forward to full take-off power. It was the last lift-off the VC-10 would ever make from British soil.

Air Force One had arrived at Riyadh at 3:33 AM local time, with the Secretary of State sound asleep in her compartment. She had wakened for a few seconds when the aircraft gently touched down and the power came off, but she had gone back to sleep immediately.

The Middle East Arms Limitations meeting with the Soviets had gone quite well. At the luncheon, Chairman Yaroslav did indeed try to drink her under the table, but Secretary Swift knew the trick that allowed the Soviets to stay on their feet long after naive Westerners collapsed in a heap. Immediately before leaving the embassy to go to the luncheon, she had eaten a quarter of a loaf of bread, plain, no butter. The calories must be watched. During the reception and the luncheon, she joined her Russian hosts in taking some bread each time she was offered a glass of vodka. The unknowing drinker who takes the vodka straight on an empty stomach very quickly becomes drunk, since the alcohol goes directly into the blood stream. The bread soaks up the vodka as it enters the stomach and then allows it to enter the blood stream slowly. Both kinds of drinkers become drunk if they drink the same amount of vodka; but the non-bread eater becomes an instant inebriate while the eater is still in control.

The principal result of the MEAL meeting was the Soviet

agreement with the United States that it was in the interests of world peace that there be a limit to the arms purchased, acquired, and located in the Middle East. It was true that the Arabs were quite capable of turning against each other as well as against Israel; and that Iran, which had become excessively militaristic under the Shah, might make a bid to conquer all of the Arab nations east of the Suez, taking over their oil riches. Chairman Yaroslav speculated that if this was indeed the Shah's long-range intent, he could probably soften the Soviets by leaving Egypt out of his net. At the same time he could pacify the Americans by by-passing Israel while promising to protect the Israelis against the Arabs.

When the MEAL meeting had examined the aircraft, tank, and artillery inventories in the Middle East, from Iran through Egypt, there was much headshaking and concern. If it was agreed that the United States and the Soviet Union would refuse to supply the Middle East nations with more than the quantities they possessed as of July 5, there would still be an effective market there for the Soviet Union and the United States, particularly for replacement of aircraft being written off by a high rate of accidents.

The MEAL discussion had concluded with a decision to have the appropriate American and Soviet staffs work out a formula to be considered at the next Strategic Arms Limitations Talks (SALT) meeting scheduled for mid-August.

Yaroslav himself, much taken with this articulate, attractive woman, escorted Jessica Swift to the airport, sitting close to her in the big black limousine, talking animatedly through the ever-present interpreter. Quite properly, the Secretary of State was flattered by this attention.

It also pleased the President of the United States. The American Ambassador, who in his own chauffeur-driven vehicle had followed the Secretary and the Chairman out to the airport, reported directly to the President as soon as he got

BALANCE OF FORCES

	manpower	planes	tanks	artillery
Egypt	650,000	600	2,500	2,000
Syria	150,000	500	2,000	600
Iraq	100,000	250	1,500	700
Jordan	80,000	75	500	600
TOTAL ARAB	980,000	1,425	6,500	3,900
Israel	400,000	430	3,000	900

back to the embassy. He was also able to report to the President that Yaroslav, his tongue loosened by vodka, had told the Secretary of State that he was delighted with the chaos in Great Britain. The Soviet Union expected that the government of the United Kingdom would be overthrown. In the meantime, the Russians were sitting back in the bushes, watching.

Before Secretary Swift departed Moscow, the U.S. Ambassador to Saudi Arabia had informed his counterpart in Moscow that the King would be pleased to receive the Secretary of State. He would expect her at ten on Tuesday morning. The King had other important meetings, but for Mrs. Swift he would set them aside.

"After all," he told the ambassador, "how could I refuse. The secretary is half Arab. Her predecessor was Jewish. She is a beautiful woman and my eye is not so old that I cannot perceive enjoyment from beholding such a lady. Also she strives mightily for peace in the Middle East and she is the representative of the President of the United States. I would see her any time, Your Excellency, any time."

At 9:45 the King's enormous air-conditioned Rolls Royce appeared at the foot of the steps of Air Force One. At ten o'clock, Secretary Swift entered the receiving room of the palace. The King, alone, was standing in front of the elaborately carved throne-like chair which he often sat in to receive supplicants, ambassadors, people wanting to do business with Saudi Arabia, and the countless host of others who sought this man's attention. He was undoubtedly the richest individual on earth, who single-handedly controlled the largest known reserves of oil in the world. His country possessed little military strength, and his nation was very small, with only eleven million people. Yet because he was the most powerful, most respected, wealthiest of all of the oil-rich Middle East Arab leaders, this monarch had enormous power in influencing the actions and policies of other Arab nations. More than any other person, he could persuade them to act in concert when it was in their collective best interests.

But not always. In 1975, contrary to the King's wishes, the emirs of Abu Dhabi and Dubai, faced with reduced buying by the consumer nations because of high prices, broke the OPEC Cartel Agreement, selling their oil at a much reduced price. This act had bent the solid quasi-monopoly front of OPEC and sent the prices downward. That momentary aberration had been dealt with by the King and his influential brother, the Crown Prince. They had told the rulers of Abu Dhabi and Dubai that if they persisted in knocking down the prices for their crude oil beyond a given base, Saudi Arabia and the other Arab oil-producing countries would place an embargo on oil shipments to any nation which was then buying oil from Abu Dhabi and Dubai. As he had pointed out to the emirs, the effect of such an embargo would be that those consuming nations would be compelled to stop buying from Abu Dhabi and Dubai immediately. Both emirates had returned forthwith to the OPEC fold.

And such was the power of this man that he could and was in the process of destroying the economy of the United Kingdom, a nation he knew to be especially vulnerable, with its massive, increasing balance of payments deficits, its long- and short-term indebtedness to the world, its failing productivity, and its high unemployment. Yes, he knew he had the power to destroy. He was prepared to use it ruthlessly against the enemies of the Arab world, and as of now the United Kingdom was an enemy. Up until this time, Great Britain had been a friend of the Arabs, except for that disastrous intervention in the Suez in the 1950's. Britain was the place where most of the young Arabian sheiks, princes, and men of royal family were educated; there were close emotional ties. The British, whose economy had increasingly been supported by Arab investments, had put a knife into the heart of their Arab friends. Now they would pay.

His robes flowing majestically, the King moved forward across the room with both hands outstretched to greet Jessica Swift. His smooth round face beamed and his black eyes were bright. The King's hawk-like nose, black moustache and goatee, and Arabic headdress made his appearance reminiscent of that of his assassinated brother.

Taking both of Jessica's hands in his, he kissed her lightly on both cheeks, bending slightly to do so. "Madam Secretary, your being here is an unexpected delight. Allah has been truly good to me this morning by opening the heavens to bring you like a dove of peace to my palace."

Still holding her hands, he stood back and appraised this superior woman, dressed in a simple white cotton dress. The Secretary returned his smile, a rare demonstration from this man. "Your Majesty flatters me in excess."

"I flatter you not at all, Madam Secretary." The King turned and led her to the long sofa against the wall next to his usual chair. "Come, we will have coffee and you will explain to me exactly why you are here."

As they sat down on the sofa, she said, "Your Majesty, I would be more naive than usual if I did not believe you understand full well exactly why I am here."

He was pleased. "Now it is you who flatters. Yes, your Ambassador was suitably vague about the reason for your visit, but you can have only one purpose in mind." The King noticed that her eyes were looking above and behind him. He, too, turned to look at the object of her gaze, then back to her. "Ah yes, you like my falcon? I have just acquired him. We are training to hunt together."

"It's a gorgeous bird. What kind is it?"

"It is a rare bird, in fact there are very few of them left in the world. It is called a peregrine falcon. This one comes from your continent, from Canada. Its summer nesting grounds are, as I am told, in an area called the Northwest Territories. This one came from near a place called Baker Lake according to the man who has acquired it for me. Evidently the Canadian government prohibits their capture, so this one obviously has come to me through a poacher. Pity, but then I will care for this bird extremely well and it will give me much pleasure. Already it has shown signs of being truly outstanding as a hunter."

"Like its master." The Secretary of State did not miss the opportunity.

While they talked, a servant poured the coffee, black, powerful, in tiny cups, as is the custom.

The King sipped with some noise as he listened to the Secretary speak. For all his interest in her as an attractive woman, he admired her far more for her shrewd wisdom, her vast knowledge of the people and affairs of the Middle East – and, for that matter, the world – and for her enormous ability as a negotiator, a trader, a quality which he attributed to her Arabic stock. Quite apart from her femininity, she was a person of superior knowledge and intellect, even more capable than her illustrious Jewish predecessor. If anyone in the world could induce him through logic and suasion to reverse his hard decision against the United Kingdom, it would be this person. The Secretary of State would be a challenge. The King would try to listen without intervening.

"Your Majesty, the President personally requested me to attend upon you. I bring you greetings from him and best wishes for your continued good health and success in all things."

The King nodded his acknowledgement.

"My government is deeply concerned that there may be disastrous consequences not only for the United Kingdom, but for western Europe and the United States, indeed the entire Western world, as a result of the action you and your Arab brothers have taken against the United Kingdom. As you know, your decision to withdraw your investments in the United Kingdom's banking system and to cut off further British investment has already forced the government to shut down all its banks and financial institutions. Overnight, London has ceased to function as the world's most important money exchange outside of New York. You have bankrupted the U.K.; the value of the pound has been cut in half; there will be critical shortages of food; and of course, your refusal to continue to supply crude oil in itself will be a disaster."

The King sat looking at her impassively, occasionally sipping loudly on the coffee.

"It is apparent to my government that unless Your Majesty can be persuaded to soften your position against the U.K., the entire economy of the Western world can be thrown into a catastrophic depression. Of course, a depression would mean that the demand for crude oil would be substantially cut. The money you are paid for your commodity would be worth a great deal less, and at the same time, inflation would not abate in any way. Therefore, the harmful effects of your action would come full circle and in fact operate in a manner detrimental to Saudi Arabia and all oil-producing Arab countries."

The King, try as he might, could not restrain himself. He raised his right hand regally to signal his intervention.

"Madam Secretary, please. I understand very well that the consequences of our action, which amount to a double boycott of the U.K.: first of the investment funds that have kept their economy alive, and second, of crude oil. This blow against Britain is obviously a retaliation for their blow against us. Selling missiles to Israel was contrary to our specific injunction against any further sales. Our action need not bring about bankruptcy if the British handle the situation with wisdom and with foresight. They ought to have made crisis arrangements long ago. My advisers tell me that if appropriate contingency-funding had been arranged against what *The Economist** calls – and has been calling for some years – 'emergency crisis day,' then our action will not cause bankruptcy. On the contrary, it will force the United Kingdom to rationalize its economy, its ability to produce, its ability to sustain the number of people that live on the Islands now. Our action will bring the malaise of Britain to a head.

"On the other hand, it is true that the parliamentary democracy system in the United Kingdom may now be obsolete, may now be unable to respond effectively to a crisis of this kind. And it may well be, therefore, that the United Kingdom will be thrown into a state of true bankruptcy. If that does happen, if there is massive unemployment – as indeed there is now – if there are shortages of food, and if there is a collapse of the economy, the Prime Minister of the United Kingdom has only himself to blame. He knew or ought to have known the risks involved when he acted contrary to my injunction and permitted the shipment of arms to Israel. The responsibility rests with him, not with me."

The Secretary took up the argument. "I can follow your line of reasoning very well, Your Majesty. But there is one point I have difficulty with. Over the years, you have purchased billions of dollars worth of fighter aircraft and missiles from the United States, while at the same time, the United States has been selling those same commodities to Israel. But you have continued to supply oil to the United States, and you have not taken any retaliatory action against us. Why do you make the distinction between the United States' supplying arms to Israel and Great Britain's doing so?"

* A prestigious British financial periodical

The King was becoming restless. The Secretary's questions were probing, too sensitive. But he controlled his impatience because he knew, with all the intuitive wisdom that Allah had bestowed upon him, that this clever, learned person knew what his answer would be before she put the question and therefore knew it would not be offensive in the asking.

"My dear Secretary, you know the answer to the question you have asked, but let me confirm it to you. It is impossible to equate our relationship with the United States with our relationship with Great Britain."

A servant entered with fresh coffee, which was poured without asking. Both the King and the Secretary were entirely oblivious of the steward.

"Our relationship with the United States, while frequently strained because you have traditionally supported Israel, is essentially one of trade and commerce. It is the trading of a commodity in which, with our OPEC partners, we have a virtual monopoly. Let us call it a *de facto* monopoly. On the other hand, the United States has in the Western industrial world a virtual *de facto* monopoly on a commodity which we badly need, and that is first-line fighter aircraft *available quickly* and with backup maintenance and resupply support. Certainly we could buy fighter aircraft from our good friend, France, but not in large numbers. Or we could attempt to do business with the Soviet Union, but in a relationship with the communists, I perceive a threat to me and my own position as an absolute monarch. There would be an intrusion into my country by Soviet technicians and support people which I would find totally unacceptable. No, we must do business with the United States for air armaments. Your country can produce high-quality aircraft in large numbers and quickly. And the United States must have our oil."

The King paused for a moment and picked up his cup. He took a quiet sip as he collected his thoughts. Then he went on, holding the tiny cup and saucer. "Furthermore, the purchase of these armaments from the United States gives us an opportunity to recycle, as the popular saying is, recycle the American dollars we have earned, a task that is becoming increasingly difficult for us. And so, if the Americans continue to support Israel, as they have been for some years now, while they at the same time supply us with aircraft and weapons we cannot acquire in our perceived time frame from any other source, well, then it is a matter which we in our wisdom accept."

The King put down his cup and saucer. The subject of Great Britain's actions was an emotional one, and he gestured emphatically as he talked.

"On the other hand, Madam Secretary, you know very well that our relationship with Great Britain is on a completely different footing. For decades, Britain has been our cultural and economic window on the West. Our young men have been educated there at London, Cambridge, Eton, Oxford, and Glasgow. It is true that of late we have been sending a few to the United States, but basically the United Kingdom has been our mentor in these matters. The British presence, both militarily and economically, has been very strong in the Middle East during most of this century. They have given us what military traditions we have, even from the time of Glub Pasha and the much fabled Lawrence. You see, there has been a close bond, a close association between the Arab nations of the Middle East and Great Britain.

"In recent years – especially after the October War in 1973 when the OPEC countries quadrupled our prices within a year – we have found ourselves with surplus revenue in our hands, in a scale of billions upon billions. All this you know. Now, what we did was to recognize that while we could invest our money, that is to say, the Arab countries could invest their new found surpluses in the United States and western Europe, yes, even in Japan, we decided to concentrate the placing of our investment monies through the London international banking system and as well through New York. We put money into London even though we recognized that the U.K. was beginning to run some major trade deficits, particularly because of its oil payments, which recently have been running in excess of three-quarters of a billion dollars a month. Their overall trade deficit sometimes reaches a billion dollars a month. In other words, without the infusion of our money, recycling if you will, the prospect of the United Kingdom's going bankrupt was, in fact, very real.

"Now, Madam Secretary, notwithstanding the precarious position of the British economy, the Arab OPEC nations, with Saudi Arabia in the vanguard, invested our money heavily into the United Kingdom, into British companies, into equities, into real estate, and into the banking system. I repeat, we did not have to invest in England. There are other places where our money could have gone, and of course, I think of the United States particularly. But we chose to stay with our friends in London, we deliberately put our money into Great Britain in order to assist the people of that nation, to prevent their economy from collapsing – twenty-one billion dollars in 1974 and even more in 1975. The British government knew we were going out of our way to help them, that we were taking enormous risks, notwithstanding the extremely high incidence of strikes, the minimal productivity of the country, and the sky-rocketing inflation. What was it – 25 per cent in 1974? Then 27 per cent in 1975? A total of 52 per cent in two years! And the rate since 1975 has been no better."

Secretary Swift broke in. "Then I suppose you believe the British have an obligation to you for investing in their economy, for sustaining it, for preventing them from going bankrupt?"

The King nodded vigorously. "Precisely. They have a moral obligation to us, and an economic obligation. In consideration of both obligations, I advised Sands that it would be inappropriate for the British government to supply to Israel any further armaments of any kind, tanks, missiles, guns, or whatever."

"Because of their obligation to you?"

"Exactly. Having advised the Prime Minister that any further sales of British armaments to Israel were unacceptable to us, I fully expected him to comply."

"But," Secretary Swift interjected, "no matter how you put the injunction to Sands, no matter what diplomatic language you use, surely it was an infringement on the sovereignty of the United Kingdom, an infringement backed up by an implied threat that you would take economic sanctions if there was failure to comply."

The King protested. "No, no. I never went that far. I never said to him, 'You do this or else.' Never. That would be . . ."

"Blackmail?"

The response was a grimace. "That is a hard, a harsh word. No, I merely pointed out the moral and economic obligations. I at no time . . ."

The Secretary had found her argument. The King was a proud man who believed himself to be honourable above all men. The word "blackmail," the act of blackmail, to him was loathsome.

"Your Majesty, you may find what I have to say harsh and unacceptable, but I have no choice. It is the belief of my government that Prime Minister Sands was blackmailed and that his refusal to accede to the blackmail, to give in to the inherent threat of reprisal should he fail to comply with your order, was a decision properly taken by a sovereign nation. The Arab nations carried out an oil boycott against the Western world after the October War of 1973. You used the

125

boycott as a weapon of war. Your threat, and now the implementation of that threat, is deemed also to be an act in support of the military advantage of all of the Arab world. It is therefore comparable to the oil boycott of 1973. You have used blackmail tactics, Your Majesty."

The absolute monarch of Saudi Arabia was furious. He stood up, drawing himself to his full height, hands clenched, fists at his side. His eyebrows arched and his eyes showed his anger. He said in an icy voice, "Madam Secretary, what you are saying is a personal affront to me. You insult me in my own palace."

Secretary Swift rose quickly to meet him almost eye to eye. "I intend no personal insult or affront, Your Majesty, but I am under obligation to my government to inform you of the opinion which is held of you as a result of your action against the United Kingdom. It is an opinion which is now worldwide."

"That I blackmailed Sands? Impossible. It is not true. It is simply not true. At no time did I threaten him. There was never any threat. It was simply that when he acted, I too acted, because he has struck a blow at the heart of the Arab world, against his friends, his Arab friends, who have sustained his nation over the years."

He turned away from her to gaze upon his falcon as he spoke, more subdued now. "I would be less than candid if I did not admit that my reputation as a leader among my own people, among all the Arab countries, is important to me. Perhaps it is the most important thing I have. I have everything else. Absolutely everything, even my health, power, riches. My reputation, how other men see me, how other countries see me, my place in history, what I can do for my people – these are things of the soul, of the spirit. There is no doubt the action I have taken against the United Kingdom is punitive. It is retaliatory. Perhaps I acted too quickly, too much on the spur of my emotion. I can also tell you that in my heart of hearts I did not believe that our action in withdrawing our money and investments from the United Kingdom would in fact precipitate a calamity, certainly not a disaster of the scale that is developing. I did not expect the British to bungle things as badly as they have. Closing down their international banking system was an incredible error. I cannot conceive of such a step, notwithstanding our run on the banks and the run by the ordinary depositors. However, what is done is done, praise Allah. But to be called a blackmailer . . . " He turned to face her as he asked the question. "What is it that you want of me?"

"Compassion. Understanding. The turning of the other cheek instead of an eye for an eye. What I ask is that you give consideration to rescinding your decision to withdraw your support from the British economy. Their banking system is shut down until Thursday – it cannot stay closed much longer. If you were to make the decision to remain with Great Britain, and to negotiate with the government for terms and conditions upon which you would be prepared to invest in their system as you have in the past, in other words, by protocol or agreement, not by unilateral threat or order on your part, then part of the harm that has been done – not all, by any means – can be overcome. It is my opinion, Your Majesty, that if you do not relent, you will have been responsible for driving Britain not only into bankruptcy, but into anarchy and into the hands of the communists."

The King moved to her, took her right hand in both of his. He spoke softly. "You give me much to think on, Madam Secretary. Before you arrived I had planned to hear you out politely, but my mind was made up. What is the American saying? 'My mind's made up, don't confuse me with the facts.' But you have confused me with the facts, and perhaps with a

127

spark of the compassion of which you speak. I will discuss with my brother and my ministers the request you have made on behalf of your government. If I am prepared to meet your request, you will hear from me before the sun sets tomorrow evening. If you do not hear from me, it will mean that my original decision is unchanged."

He bent to kiss her hand. Then, as he lifted his head, he gave her gentle words of farewell. "Allah be with you."

"And with Your Majesty."

10:55 AM
Baker Lake, Northwest Territories
Canada

The VC-10's flight across the Atlantic had been smooth and uneventful, the large, swept-wing jet touching down in bright sunlight on the runway at Frobisher Bay at 7:35 AM local time. The weather had closed in at Goose Bay making it necessary to use the alternate airport at Frobisher Bay.

On the way across the Atlantic several messages had been passed to the Prime Minister for consideration and reply. Hobson, in Washington, had come up with a proposal that he wanted to put to the Americans concerning oil supply and financing, but Sands had vetoed it out of hand. In fact, the impracticality of Hobson's idea alarmed Sands and underscored the decision that he himself should take part in the Washington conference. He started to make arrangements to get there earlier than scheduled. He even considered instructing Squadron Leader Robins to divert to Washington instead of going on to Vancouver, but decided to continue with his plan to get the meeting with the Prime Minister of Canada out of the way.

A message had come from Stanton advising that there was

a mass rally underway at the industrial city of Manchester and another at Glasgow, but that none of the known communist agitators were present at these gatherings, which appeared to be peaceful. Also the TUC request to all member unions or constituent unions to work and forego strikes had been successful. All strikes in the United Kingdom had been abandoned, all bargaining sessions had been postponed and the TUC itself had suggested a temporary formula of compulsory arbitration in the settlement of all current wage disputes.

Another message arrived from Stanton when the Prime Minister's aircraft was about forty-five minutes out of Frobisher Bay, advising that the U.S. Secretary of State was now due back in Washington from Moscow at 6:00 PM Washington time. She had been diverted to Saudi Arabia by the President to pursue the possibility of softening the hard line the Arabs had taken against the U.K. The President did not want to open the conference with the British until the Secretary was present. The meeting was therefore now scheduled to get underway at eight that evening, Washington time. This news gave the Prime Minister considerable relief. If his luck held out, he could be into the Washington meeting shortly after it began and he could take the negotiations out of Hobson's hands.

The refueling stop at Frobisher had taken two hours. There was trouble with the ground fuel-pumping system which had finally been repaired. The Prime Minister had been met formally by the local administrator, who insisted on giving him and Prentice a fast tour of the community. Sands had expected the temperature to be cold and to find snow on the ground but there was none to be seen. The temperature was a balmy 72°F.* under the high summer sun of the Arctic,

* 22°Celsius

as he and his host bounced in a van through the Eskimo village to the east of the airport.

Sands was taken aback by what he regarded to be the squalor and primitive conditions under which these native people existed. The housing was of thin frame construction, obviously built by the white man without any understanding of the needs of the people or the environment in which they had to live. Refuse littered the area. He asked the local administrator what had happened to the hundreds and millions of dollars that were spent each year by the Department of Indian Affairs and Northern Development for the native people. The reply was that the native people don't look after the things that are given to them, to which the Prime Minister responded that he couldn't see that they had been given anything.

Back down on the airstrip, Sands had been impressed by the multi-storey highrise apartment and commercial tower which had been built primarily to meet the needs of the itinerant travellers from the south and the civil servants who were stationed at Frobisher. He decided it would not be appropriate to make comment on the contrast that was obvious between the accommodation provided for the Eskimo and that for the white man. When he asked if the Eskimo community was typical of native communities across the Northwest Territories, the answer was yes, even at the capital city, Yellowknife, and at the new community of Inuvik in the Mackenzie delta.

Just before startup of the VC-10 at 9:32 AM, Squadron Leader Robins showed the Prime Minister the proposed route to Vancouver which he had drawn on an aircraft position chart. On departing Frobisher, they would climb to 30,000 feet, which would be their cruising altitude, across the northern sector of Hudson Bay, just south of Southampton Island, over Rankin Inlet on the west coast of Hudson Bay,

131

passing just about forty miles south of Baker Lake, then to Uranium City, near the Athabasca Tar Sands, then into Vancouver International at 11:35 hours local time, much in advance of the time Sands had expected. Sands was pleased; he could get his meeting with Roussel over with earlier than he expected and be on his way to Washington.

Robins also mentioned that they had an unserviceable weather radar-scope. "But," he was quick to add, "it shouldn't be any problem with good weather at altitude all the way."

As planned, the VC-10 lifted off from Frobisher at 9:45 AM, with full fuel on board, then turned west on course climbing through to 30,000 feet. The Prime Minister, alert and refreshed by the two to three hours of sleep he had been able to catch on the way across the Atlantic, was fascinated by the magnificent view outside of the aircraft as they approached Hudson Bay. The visibility was unlimited. The sky was clear of all cloud, except for the anvil tops of a line of thunder clouds far ahead.

In the cockpit of the VC-10, Squadron Leader Robins and his crew, uniform jackets off for comfort, constantly monitored the instruments of the aircraft, which had been placed on auto-pilot control, or "George" as the RAF called it. All engine instruments were reading normal. The flight was totally routine and typically well managed.

Ahead Robins could see the top of the line of thunderstorm clouds sitting in the middle of Hudson Bay, soaking up water to feed their violent internal wind/rain/hail/snow-filled and electrically charged systems, generated by a hot sun and warm air passing over the cold surface of the bay.

"We'll miss that monster ahead of us," Robins remarked to his co-pilot, Cranston.

"Should be two or three miles south of it," Cranston agreed.

Ahead of the VC-10, perhaps fifteen miles by Robins' estimate, and at his level, sat the flat spread-out white head of a huge cumulonimbus thundercloud, its forerunning tentacles of thin but thickening cloud reaching out toward them. On their present course they would pass through the advance cloud but avoid the dangerous main column. There should be no problem. The VC-10 was about ten miles east of the thunderhead when it entered the advance cloud.

Suddenly it was as if a million machine-gun bullets had hit the huge aircraft at the same instant. It was like an explosion. The noise was deafening.

"Hail!" Robins screamed as in a second he disengaged the auto-pilot and turned the wheel hard to the left. He used both hands to haul back on the control column to get out of the lethal white shroud of ice missiles spewing out of the volcanic top of the thundercloud. Then he made a harsh pullback on the throttles to cut the engines back to idle. Large hailstones ingested into the delicately balanced spinning blades of a jet engine could cause irreparable damage.

To Robins it seemed like an eternity until the aircraft broke clear of the deceptive, deadly cloud of hailstones. In fact it was no more than five seconds before the VC-10 burst out into the clear, sun-filled blue sky. But during those short seconds the machine had taken a dreadful hammering. The nose cone was battered in, as were the leading edges of the wings, elevators, and the fin. The windscreen had not caved in under the tremendous beating but was shattered into a million cracks. It was opaque; the crew could not see through it.

The engines! Robins had no other thought now except for engine damage. His fast action in reducing power to idle may have saved the jets. Before he attempted to return to cruise-power he would have to use extreme care. Slowly he eased all four throttles to quarter-power, anxiously monitoring his engine instruments. Immediately he could feel and hear a thumping from the tail section where the four huge engines were located.

Co-pilot Cranston shouted. "JPT* is increasing to limits in both starboard engines and inner port!" That meant trouble – compressor surging and internal damage to those three engines. That was where the thumping was coming from.

"Shut down inner port and both starboard!" Robins' command was cool and quiet as all three officers worked furiously to stop the three damaged engines. Ominously the whine of the jets began to disappear as the fuel was cut. The thumping ceased as the engines died.

"Now, chaps, a small prayer for the outboard port engine." Robins muttered as he watched the Jet Pipe Temperature instrument for the remaining power plant. "It's holding steady. I'll take her up to half-power." Gently he eased the throttle up to half. JPT steady. No thumping. "Now to full-power."

At full-power the lone engine held steady. Miraculously it had escaped damage. At least there was no indication of harm. But with only one engine left, Robins had no choice. The aircraft could not keep flying. He would have to force-land. The best he could hope for was that the one engine would allow him to maintain a safe rate of descent just before touchdown, wherever that would be.

"Shut off all navigation aids, everything that uses electricity except the VHF**set," was Robins' next command. "The generator from our live engine can't carry the load."

The VC-10 was now descending at 1,000 feet a minute. Robins could hold it there with an air speed of 150 knots. He

* Jet Pipe Temperature
** VHF – Very High Frequency radio transmitter and receiver

had put it on its westerly course after his violent pullout from the hail cloud.

"Jason, where are we?" Robins asked.

Flight Engineer Jason Rupert replied swiftly. "We're about fifty miles east of Chesterfield Inlet. We should be able to see the shoreline any minute now."

"Not out of this windscreen," Robins responded sarcastically, as he turned the VHF selection knob to the Chesterfield Inlet frequency of 341. To his first officer Robins said, "Go to emergency frequency and give a MAYDAY report. I'll talk to Chesterfield Inlet."

He pushed his transmitter button. "Chesterfield Inlet, this is Ascot 1105, a Royal Air Force VC-10. I have an emergency. Do you read?"

The reply was immediate. "VC-10. Read you 5 and 5. Go."

"Chesterfield, I have three engines out. Preparing to force-land. I am forty-five miles east of you at 20,000 feet. What are your conditions."

There was a slight pause.

"VC-10, we have a zero-zero weather condition here with advection fog moving in off Hudson Bay. Suggest you try Baker Lake area. It may have clear patches. Baker Lake is also zero-zero but it has too short a strip for you anyway. But you might get a break in the fog if you can get further inland."

"Okay, Chesterfield. We'll head inland. Will you advise Baker Lake I'll be talking to them shortly?"

"Wilco."

Fog. Robins would have to land the VC-10 blind, in terrain he knew nothing about – the most terrifying kind of forced landing conceivable. He looked over at Cranston, who had finished his MAYDAY message and had been listening to Robins' conversation with Chesterfield Inlet. Cranston's eyes were wide with fear.

It was the expression in Cranston's eyes that helped Robins control his own rising panic. He turned back to his instruments. He was passing through 19,000 feet.

"Cranston, go back and tell the Prime Minister and Prentice to prepare for a crash-landing. Don't tell them we're going to do it blind. Make sure they're strapped in. Tell them to bend forward as soon as we enter cloud."

Cranston unstrapped the safety harness and moved quickly out of the flight compartment.

As the VC-10 passed through 10,000 feet Robins kept the airspeed at 150 knots and his rate of descent at 1,000 feet a minute. Ten minutes to go to touchdown.

He peered out the side window of the cockpit. It had escaped the destructive force of the hail and would be his only means of judging his landing, if in fact he was lucky enough to find a break in the fog. Robins called Baker Lake, got a reply, then asked, "Baker Lake, what is your terrain like? What's the land like? Is it mountainous, are there trees?"

"VC-10, the land to the southeast of Baker Lake is flat but slightly rolling tundra. There are no trees. There are many small lakes. The ground is rock-strewn, but the rocks are small. There are some eskers, that is, gravel ridges, which rise five to ten feet above the terrain. At Baker Lake we have a series of low hills, which I suggest you stay away from. I recommend you stay south of Baker Lake. That'll put you into the flattest area around here."

"Roger, Baker Lake," Robins acknowledged.

Cranston returned to the cockpit, giving a thumbs-up sign indicating he had briefed the Prime Minister.

Robins said, "We'll jettison all our fuel except 4,500 pounds." Cranston nodded and commenced the jettison operation. "Baker Lake, VC-10. What's your altimeter reading?" Robins asked.

"Three zero point one seven."

Robins automatically adjusted his altimeter, which now indicated 7,100 feet. His map showed the area south of Baker Lake to be fifty feet above sea level, which should be the reading on his altimeter when contact with the ground was made. He switched to intercom. "Right. We'll descend at 1,000 feet a minute until just before we hit fog, then I'll pull it back to 130 knots – just above stalling speed with the rate of descent of no more than a hundred feet a minute. Full flap. The gear will remain up. Impact at a descent of a hundred feet a minute should be smooth as silk. As soon as the aircraft comes to a halt on the ground, everybody out through the front emergency door. We can't take any chances in case we burn, so it's up to you two and the crewmen to get the P.M. out that bloody door the instant we stop."

He asked for and received an acknowledgement from the two crewmen strapped in their seats at the rear of the VC-10.

The squadron leader kept talking, mainly to reassure himself. "This will be just like a glassy water landing in a float plane. You can't see the surface of the water so fly it in on the dials, just above stalling speed with a rate of descent between fifty and one hundred feet a minute with power on, and when you touch the water, you pull off the power. That's the technique we'll use today, chaps."

Robins could not see him, but Cranston was shaking with fear. Flight Engineer Rupert had moved back into the cabin, strapped himself in the second seat from the front bulkhead, then bent forward in a crouched position waiting for the impact.

There was no break in the fog below. The VC-10 rapidly approached the thick white blanket. Just above it, Robins carried out his final landing procedures: flaps down, engine full bore, speed five knots above stall, tail way down. Then he was into the blinding solid fog as his altimeter passed the 350-foot mark. Robins kept the nose up and held a rate of descent

THE ROUTE OF THE VC-10

GREENLAND

Southampton Island

Frobisher Bay

London →

Chesterfield Inlet

...kin Inlet

Hudson Bay

LABRADOR

NEWFOUNDLAND

ONTARIO

QUEBEC

Timmins •

Quebec •

NOVA SCOTIA

—N—

0   100   200   300   400   500   miles

of seventy-five feet per minute. The aircraft was as steady as a rock as the squadron leader felt his way to the unknown, unseen ground. If the instruments were right, at any time after the altimeter showed one hundred feet contact would be made with the tundra and it would be all over.

The altimeter needle showed one hundred feet. Robins was shaking from head to toe; his heart was beating wildly. Instinctive, uncontrollable animal fear seized him. His shaking left hand held the wheel on the control column and his right hand gripped the throttle lever of the port engine, prepared to pull it back on the instant of impact.

That instant came as the needle touched the eighty-foot mark. The tail, well down during the descent, hit the ground first, giving off a high-pitched scream as the huge aluminum machine was clawed by the loose rocks of the tundra. At that second, Robins overcame his instinct to pull back further on the control column. He hauled the power off. He could feel the aircraft settle. The impact caused the tail to act like a fulcrum, throwing the front end of the machine to the ground. The noise of scraping, wrenching, tearing, and ripping was deafening as the smooth, curved, beautifully contoured machine was disembowelled. It bounced and lurched, grinding its way across the boulder-strewn tundra, buffeting the people inside it unmercifully.

Robins and Cranston, lashed to their seats by tight shoulder straps, attempted to shield their faces with their arms. Had they attempted to look out the side windows of the cockpit, they would not have been able to see through the thick fog to the ground beneath them.

Still travelling at high speed – Robins made a guess at about 60 knots – the grinding, screeching noise ended for a second as the aircraft went over a ridge, then dropped down with a thundering crash which broke off the entire tail section from a point about fifteen feet ahead of the fin.

On and on hurtled the VC-10. Robins thought it would never stop. Or if it did, it would do so suddenly, ramming into the face of a ridge such as the one they had just passed over, a crashing stop that would certainly kill them all.

4:20 PM
10 Downing Street
London, England

The Acting Prime Minister, Peter Stanton, sat with his telephone pressed against his left ear, a hank of straight, long, grey-brown hair falling over his pale forehead. He listened intently, incredulously, to the clipped words of the Secretary of Defence, Lord John Cutting. Another riot, this time in Manchester. Fifteen people killed, countless injured. Troops had used only the usual rubber bullets, tear gas, electric prodders, fire hoses, but there had been hand-to-hand fighting. It was communist-organized and communist-led, no doubt about that. The leaders were easily identified.

"My people report that crowds are gathering at this very moment in Glasgow and Liverpool and again right here in London. This time in Leicester Square." Lord John Cutting's voice was hard and determined. "Peter, I have no choice but to recommend to you in your capacity as Acting Prime Minister that martial law be decreed as quickly as possible. We must bring this situation under control and let the people know we mean business. If we don't, we're looking down the throat of a revolution!"

"I think you'd better make your recommendation to Cabinet, John," Stanton replied. "We're due to get underway in ten minutes, at 4:30. You should bring with you the Chief of Defence Staff and whatever other bodies you consider appropriate in case Cabinet has any questions. I'll try to get hold of the Prime Minister. It's imperative that we get his opinion."

"I don't know why the hell he went to North America anyway," Cutting complained. "He should have stayed here at the centre of things instead of thrashing off all over the bloody world!"

"We've been all through that, John. The Prime Minister's priority is people and the salvation of the economy, riots or no riots. It was the opinion of Cabinet, and you were there, that he should go to North America to see the President, to get the Americans' financial support for food, and to secure their help in getting a continuing supply of crude oil. There is no way out of this without the Americans. We're not going to get their support merely by sending them telegrams, notes, or communications through our Ambassador. It just won't wash."

Cutting would not give up. "But why in heaven's name would he go to Canada first? What can the Canadians do for us?"

"Not much, except take all of our people who want to go there. As I understand it, Jeremy thought he could see the Canadian Prime Minister first, get that over with quickly and then double back to Washington for the important meetings, really important meetings, with the President and the Secretary of State. The emigration matter is very important to him as you know, because his concern is for people. He knows damn well we've got to get them off the Islands quickly. The fact is, John, he's there, or on his way there, and we're here. It's up to us to make the decisions, whether we like it or not, even if it's whether we should declare martial law or not."

The Secretary of Defence backed off. "Perhaps you're right. I shall be there directly."

Stanton, sitting at Sands' desk in the library at 10 Downing Street, immediately issued instructions to the Secretary of the Cabinet to make telephone or radio contact with the Prime Minister, wherever he was, no matter what he was doing. He had to get the Prime Minister on the line. Then Stanton placed a call to the Attorney General and requested him to be prepared to brief the Cabinet on the steps necessary to impose martial law, and the ramifications of its being put into effect. The Attorney General had anticipated such a request and had been fully briefed by his staff.

Stanton had telephoned Leader of the Opposition Thomas Short, who had decided he would not express an opinion on martial law but would leave it to the Cabinet. Stanton understood his tactic. Short would be able to criticize the government whichever way it went.

The Cabinet meeting had started promptly at 4:30, with Lord John Cutting outlining the situation in Liverpool and Manchester, as well as in London. He had many questions thrown at him by his colleagues, but none that he could not answer, so it was not necessary to bring into the meeting the Chief of Defence Staff, who had been waiting outside the Cabinet Room. Cutting had concluded his presentation by forcefully urging the imposition of martial law.

"Is there an alternative, Lord John?" It was Angus Stewart's question.

"As I see it, it is martial law or no. If no, then I tell you, we are faced with a revolution. The seeds, the ingredients, everything is there, including the communist leadership. They have a plan going now which is as clear as I can possibly put it to you. If we do not move in now, if we do not impose martial law, you will see bloodshed, violence, total anarchy, a revolution the like of which this country has never seen and

144

has never believed possible. The government, our system of government, Parliament, the whole structure will be over-thrown. That is the alternative, Mr. Stewart."

The Secretary for Scotland shot back. "That might be your opinion, sir, but it's not mine. Certainly I can, and indeed I must believe that there are huge gatherings of people in Liverpool, in Manchester, and here in London at this time, at this very moment. And indeed those gatherings are potential riot spots. But at a time of national upheaval, when the government apparently has lost the ability to act, people will naturally gather in crowds to protest, to show in some tangible way that they must be listened to, that their plight must be understood, that there must be action. And you keep saying 'communist,' Lord John. It seems to me that, as McCarthy did in the United States years and years ago, you are looking under rocks for worms which just aren't there. I know there are communists among the English and the Scottish and the Welsh and the Irish, the trade unions, among the workers. What else would you expect with working conditions, wages, the economy, the sad state of this floundering nation. I'm sure you'll see communists present at these mass rallies that are going on at this moment. But to draw from this the proposi-tion that there is a plan afoot, that there is a scheme – you haven't said it yet – but a scheme masterminded by Moscow, is, in my opinion, absolutely ridiculous.

"Scotsmen, Englishmen, everyone in Great Britain is entitled to free speech, the right to gather in public places, to protest. This is a democratic nation. It is not yet a dictatorship. But what you propose, Lord John, is to place in the hands of this government – indeed the hands of one man if you will, the hands of the Prime Minister – the first opportunity in our modern history for a dictatorship. You do that when you impose martial law. You place in the hands of the leader of the government, the Prime Minister, the ultimate military weapon with which to rule the country without reference to Parliament. I say, Acting Prime Minister, that the dangers to democracy are grave if martial law is imposed. I say that a case has not been made that will stand the test of examination beyond a reasonable doubt. That is the test this Cabinet, this government, must bring to bear on this question. I will vote, but I hope that there are many others in this Cabinet who will vote with me. I will vote against martial law when the question is put, Acting Prime Minister!''

The debate raged on. Stanton, from his vantage point as chairman, soon was able to assess that there was a virtually even split. There was still no word from the Prime Minister. God, he wished Sands were here to sort this one out.

The question was formalized when Lord John Cutting moved that martial law be decreed throughout the United Kingdom. As chairman, Stanton had no alternative but to accept the motion. It had been properly seconded by Sir Benjamin Wicks. Anticipating a split vote which would put him in the position of having to cast the deciding vote, Stanton hesitated, then said, ''I do not wish to put this question to the vote until I've had a chance to talk with the Prime Minister.'' There were nods of approval around the table. ''I don't know what the delay is. They should have been through to him by now. So perhaps we could adjourn for ten minutes.''

''We can't delay longer than that. Time is of the essence with this decision if it's going to be positively implemented,'' Cutting interjected. ''We must act immediately. If we can't raise the Prime Minister, we'll have to act without him!''

There were further indications of agreement with Cutting's position around the table from both sides in the debate.

''Very well, we'll reconvene in ten minutes.'' At that instant the door from the Secretary of the Cabinet's office burst open. The Secretary himself, all protocol and restraint gone, panic in

146

his eyes and on his face, burst into the Cabinet Room, shouting, "The Prime Minister's aircraft. It's crashed somewhere in northern Canada. They broadcast a MAYDAY signal about fifteen minutes ago. They lost three engines and had to come down. They've lost all radio contact."

Instantly there were questions thrown excitedly from all around the Cabinet table at the Cabinet Secretary. Stanton overruled all of them, shouting, "Please, ladies and gentlemen. Be calm and let Sir Peter tell us what he knows." When the noise died down, Stanton said, "Now, Sir Peter, you've said the Prime Minister's aircraft has crashed. They had sent out a MAYDAY message about fifteen minutes ago and all radio contact had been lost."

"That's correct, sir."

"Where did this report come from?"

"A radio station at a place called Rankin Inlet on the west coast of Hudson Bay. The Rankin radio operator passed them over to another station called Baker Lake, not far away. The Baker Lake operator advised them to let down in flat country to the south of Baker Lake. They've had no further radio contact since. They assume they've crash-landed."

Cutting muttered, "The chance of survival is almost nil."

Stanton ignored him. "Thank you, Sir Peter. It is absolutely imperative that the Cabinet be informed immediately of any information you receive. I would be obliged if you would instruct your staff accordingly and then rejoin us."

As the Secretary of the Cabinet turned and left the room, the Acting Prime Minister said to his colleagues, "I suggest that we press on with the vote on the motion that martial law be imposed. In the absence of the Secretary, I shall record the vote myself."

Three minutes later the Acting Prime Minister had recorded ten votes yea, and ten votes nay. His would be the deciding vote.

Stanton announced, "It's a tie. Mine will be the deciding vote. My instinct tells me to vote against the motion. But my logic, my responsibility to my country, and my conscience tell me that I must vote for the motion. As of this moment, there will be martial law throughout the United Kingdom!"

10:56 AM
Crash Site at Carr Lake
Near Baker Lake,
Northwest Territories
Canada

Slowly the huge, broken VC-10 slewed sideways. Robins could feel it slowing down quickly. In a moment the grinding, terrifying ordeal had come to an end, as the wreckage skidded to a halt with the front part of the aircraft, the cockpit and cabin area, totally intact.

For a few seconds, there was complete silence except for the incongruous whirring of the VHF radio set and the flight instruments. There had been no opportunity for either pilot to attempt to turn off any switches. Basil Robins pulled himself together, barking at Cranston, "Get all those switches off and let's get the hell out of here. If she's going to burn, she'll go any second."

Their four trained hands leaped from switch to switch as they completed the shutdown of all systems, threw off their safety harnesses and, with Robins in the lead, moved quickly into the passenger compartment. There, through the gaping hole left by the disappearance of the tail section, Rupert could be seen jumping from the floor deck and disappearing into the fog below, as he leaped the six feet from the deck to the ground.

On reaching the edge of the deck, Robins looked down and saw Rupert, Prentice, and the Prime Minister, whose face was contorted with pain as he gripped his left arm. Waving his arm frantically, Robins shouted, "Away from the aircraft! Get away from the aircraft as fast as you can! I can't tell whether we've got a fire or not. I can't even see the wings. Go about a hundred paces, then lie down flat in case she blows. And stay together. All we need is for somebody to get lost in this pea-soup."

There wasn't time to ask about the Prime Minister's arm or about the two crewmen who had been in the tail section, wherever it was. "Mason, are you all right?" Robins shouted into the fog at the top of his lungs. No reply.

Robins jumped down, followed by Cranston. The first three had already disappeared, stumbling over the stones which lay in their path. They had followed the squadron leader's instructions, flattening themselves against the ground when they were about a hundred paces away from the aircraft. There they had waited, pestered constantly by mosquitoes, for what had seemed to each of them to be an eternal length of time. Finally Robins shouted into the fog, "It's okay to go back now. The fire danger is out of the way. I'll go back first with Cranston, then I'll guide you back by voice. Prime Minister, are you all right? Can you make it back?"

From out of the solid, totally enveloping grey mist came the Prime Minister's voice. "I can make it back, Basil, but my left arm, I'm afraid it's broken."

"God!" muttered Robins as he motioned Cranston to follow him. The two of them moved off cautiously in the direction in which the squadron leader was certain, well, almost certain, the main section of the aircraft lay. His superb sense of direction did not fail him. After counting forty-eight paces, the top of his head bounced against the underside of the starboard wing tip, tilted high in the air.

He guided Sands, Prentice, and Rupert to the aircraft easily with his voice. He and Cranston then joined hands to hoist Flight Engineer Rupert up into the broken fuselage. Rupert opened the port door to the cabin just behind the cockpit. Then all the men except Sands pitched in to pile rocks against the fuselage, eventually making a set of rough steps up to the doorway. While the rocks were being piled, the squadron leader left the working party, making his way cautiously toward the spot where he guessed the severed tail section might be, probably a hundred yards back. Twice he stopped to call out for the two crewmen who had been in the rear section of the machine. Silence.

Inching through the fog, following gouge marks in the tundra which the front section of the VC-10 had made, Robins touched the aluminum skin of the tail section at the same instant he saw it. It was turned sideways and to the right, ninety degrees from the path the front section had taken. He moved carefully, feeling his way along the smooth cold metal surface until he touched the jagged edge where the aircraft had broken in two.

As he stepped around the ripped fuselage belly, Robins stopped. His face was within inches of hanging pieces of shredded blue cloth. In one ghastly moment, Robins realized they were the pant-legs of a Royal Air Force uniform, torn, soaked in blood, and empty.

Above him within the broken tail section were the crewmen, Warrant Officer Mason and Sergeant Price, still strapped side by side in their seats at the point where the VC-10 had come apart. When the aircraft had split, the rear section had moved sideways, grinding against the front part of the machine in a slicing motion which had severed both men's legs just below the knees. Battered unconscious, they had bled to death.

Appalled by his discovery, Robins slowly made his way back to the main section of the VC-10. Entering the cabin, the squadron leader tersely reported what he had found, then immediately inspected the Prime Minister's limp arm. No doubt about it, it had been broken between the elbow and the wrist when Sands had been thrown violently against a window during a vicious lunge of the aircraft. He had instinctively raised his left arm to protect himself and in the process the bone was cracked. It was not a protruding break, although the bone had separated. Robins could feel the jagged edges not far beneath the skin. It was a bad break and painful. The Prime Minister would have to have medical attention as quickly as possible.

In the meantime, the combined first-aid skills of the crew would have to do. Robins spread a blanket on the cabin floor and had the Prime Minister lie on it. He needed a flat surface to work on. Cranston broke open the well-stocked first-aid kit, producing a needle containing a pain-killing drug, and swiftly injected it into the Prime Minister's arm. Sands gritted his teeth, but uttered not one cry of pain. He had passed out.

Robins worked quickly while Sands was unconscious. He manipulated the bone back into what he considered a mesh of the two pieces, laid two splint sections alongside the arm, then gingerly wrapped an elastic surgical bandage around the splints and the injured limb.

Robins moved into the cockpit, flicked on the battery master switch to allow the activation of the radios, then turned on one of his VHF transmitter/receiver sets, which immediately whirred into life in the compartment behind the co-pilot's seat.

His first check was to make sure the Emergency Location Transmitter (ELT) had been activated by the crash and that it was functioning properly. This he did by selecting the ELT transmission frequency of 121.5. Immediately the receiver produced an ear-piercing, undulating, high-pitched whine, the universal distress call of a downed aircraft. It was this signal that would guide searching aircraft directly to the crash location.

Then came the next crucial test. If this one didn't work, it meant the Prime Minister would be out of touch with his crisis-ridden Cabinet and the leaders of the United States and Canada, the two countries which he counted on so desperately for assistance and support. Robins didn't like to think about the possibilities. Even if Search and Rescue (SAR) aircraft were airborne at that very moment, and even if they were circling overhead, no one could salvage them until that bloody fog lifted. Would it be just a few hours, a day, two days? What would happen to the government of the U.K. in this hour of chaos and disaster if the Prime Minister was to be out of touch for two critical days?

Brushing away the incessant mosquitoes as he checked that the radio frequency was still on Baker Lake, he thought to himself, "They'll have mine for bookends, and if this doesn't work, then for double bookends." As he picked up the microphone, he muttered to himself, "Dear God, let this work."

Then he pressed the transmit button. "Baker Lake, this is VC-10. Do you read me? Over."

Silence.

A sense of urgency now in the voice: "Baker Lake radio, this is VC-10. Do you read? Over."

Silence again.

But just as he was about to transmit once more, the sweet sound came to his ears loud and clear.

"VC-10, this is Baker Lake radio. Sorry to be so long. I was tied on another transmission. The whole world's calling me,

153

trying to find out what's happened to you. Where are you VC-10?"

In his calmest full-bodied, English upper-class voice, Squadron Leader Basil Robins gave his new friend and link to the world, the operator at Baker Lake radio, a full report of the events. He asked that the first communication be to the appropriate Search and Rescue unit of the Air Transport Group of the Canadian Armed Forces, so their facilities could be galvanized into action and medical attention be provided to the Prime Minister at the earliest possible moment. And the U.K. government, the President of the United States, and the Prime Minister of Canada should be informed immediately.

The Baker Lake operator acknowledged the instructions, adding, "I'll ask the Search and Rescue people at Edmonton to pass the message to London, Washington, and Ottawa. They'll know whom to contact. I sure don't."

"How long is this bloody fog going to last?"

"Probably another twenty-four hours, anyhow. We're in the middle of a high pressure area which just isn't moving at all."

"What's the closest open airfield?"

"Churchill, about 350 miles to the south. It's a big base. The SAR people will probably use it as their jumping-off point when they come in to get you."

"Have you a telephone link to the south, or do you have to communicate by radio?"

"Affirmative. We have telephone by satellite, Anik II or III, I don't know which it is."

"Right. Could you hook the telephone directly into your VHF radio system. In other words, could you arrange it so the Prime Minister could talk directly with any person?"

"Sure, no problem. Mind you, we have a lot of traffic through this shack, so there may be delays."

"Yes, of course, but there may be some extremely urgent talks the Prime Minister will have to have with people."

"Yeah, I'll bet. I heard something about the shambles in England. It must be a real mess. But I have to warn you. If any of those urgent talks are also supposed to be confidential, forget it. We have all kinds of people who listen in on the Baker Lake frequency. On top of that we're pretty certain the Russians monitor our satellite telephone transmissions and anything else they can pick up. As soon as they know the Prime Minister's aircraft is here and he's okay they'll be busting a gut to hear everything that's said. So all I'm saying is be careful what you say."

"Understood," Robins acknowledged.

The operator then cut off the conversation by saying, "I'll pass your message right away, sir, and get back to you."

The squadron leader hung the microphone on its hook, turned up the VHF radio volume so he could monitor Baker Lake radio transmissions, and then went back into the cabin. As he stopped and looked down at the prostrate, unconscious Prime Minister, Robins, in a sort of contemplative daze, muttered half to Cranston and half to himself, "It's unbelievable. On this man's shoulders rests the future of our country. And here we are a million miles from nowhere." He shook his head. "Incredible."

12:55 PM
Vancouver, British Columbia
Canada

On the way across the Atlantic, and after some discussion with André Vachon and Pierre Pratte, the Prime Minister of Canada had decided that, after stopping at Ottawa to refuel, he should go straight to Vancouver. He would arrive in that city just after midnight which would give him a chance to have a long, badly needed rest before he met the British Prime Minister around one o'clock.

The Canadian Forces 707 jet arrived at Ottawa just after 9:00 PM Monday. There, Roussel said good-bye to his wife Manon, who was anxious to get back to Sussex Drive and her children and grandchildren in Montreal. She detested political dinners and trips. Roussel did not press her to go on with him. He never did.

Finance Minister André Vachon also remained in Ottawa, with instructions from the Prime Minister to assist the Minister of Citizenship and Immigration in the preparation of information about the impact on Canada of an unknown number of British immigrants in a mass exodus from the U.K. For the Canadians, the immigration question had priority. They understood the British need for money, food, and oil, but those commodities were more easily given than was access to Canada.

Roussel could see no reason to change the time of the proposed Cabinet meeting at eight Wednesday evening, but he had considered some sort of briefing for the Cabinet on the answers to the questions posed, especially those concerning housing, the distribution of the new population across the country, and the ability of the country to absorb the new workers. Vachon had argued that this information would be of value only if the Cabinet decided to accept open-gate immigration from Great Britain. Pratte, on the other hand, had suggested that the Cabinet should have as much information as possible. Completely apart from the attitude of Quebec, there might be real reasons why Canada could not physically or economically withstand the impact of two million people in such a short period. In the end, Roussel had instructed Vachon to organize a personal briefing for the Prime Minister. It should take place at five o'clock Wednesday in the Cabinet Room in the Centre Block. Any Cabinet minister who wished to attend could do so, but it was not mandatory that they take part. Vachon's office would notify all Cabinet members. It would be interesting to see who turned up.

During the Ottawa stopover, the Prime Minister received Yves Parent, his Minister for External Affairs, who had briefed him on current developments in the United Kingdom. The pound, cut almost in half in value, was holding steady at $1.06; the banks were still closed and apparently would be until Thursday. The City of London had stopped all activities as a principal world money exchange. There were reports of mass protest gatherings at Manchester, at Liverpool, and another in London, but as yet there had been no news of the declaration of martial law by the British government.

As far as Parent could determine, all the appropriate ministries were at work on the Prime Minister's questions, and a thorough briefing could be expected at the time the Prime

157

Minister had set. An assistant to Pierre Pratte delivered to the aircraft a bulging briefcase, full of documents requiring the Prime Minister's attention or signature, and all of Monday's newspapers from Montreal, Ottawa, and Toronto. Roussel would devour these during the flight to Vancouver. It was his practice (he liked to compare himself to the late John F. Kennedy) to keep abreast of world events and of what the world and his own nation thought of him. Quite often what he saw infuriated him: a cartoon, a cutting editorial, remarks about his wife or family; but it was all part of the game, all part of the business of achieving and maintaining political power.

The Canadian Armed Forces 707 departed Ottawa within an hour after its arrival, landing at Vancouver International at 12:34 AM local time. Through a herculean effort, the Prime Minister managed to keep the bar shut during the flight and so was able to accomplish a great deal, wading through all of the newspapers and three-quarters of the material in the briefcase.

By 2:00 AM a jet-lag-exhausted Joseph Roussel climbed into bed at the Hotel Vancouver, with strict instructions to Pierre Pratte that he was not to be disturbed until noon unless some emergency occurred.

At 11:15 AM Pratte, also exhausted, and sleeping soundly in the smaller bedroom of the suite, was forced awake by the insistent ringing of the telephone. It was the hotel operator. "Sir, I know you didn't want to be disturbed except in an emergency, but I have the Minister for External Affairs, Mr. Parent, on the line. He says it's an emergency and he must speak with you."

Pratte sat up in bed, reached for his glasses on the table and for his ever-present notepad and pen. "Okay. I'll speak to him."

"Before I put you through, sir, I have another urgent call. It

158

came in about an hour ago, but I thought it could wait. Would the Prime Minister please call the Premier of British Columbia as soon as possible?'' She gave Pratte his telephone number – Oscar Bullit, the loud, flamboyant Premier of British Columbia.

Then Parent was on the line. He sounded excited. ''We've had word that Prime Minister Sands' aircraft has crashed, but so far as I can find out, he's all right. The plane's down near Baker Lake in the Northwest Territories.''

Pratte was shocked. The U.K. had enough of a disaster on its hands without this. And the aircraft was down near Baker Lake in flat, barren tundra.

''You say he's unhurt?''

Parent replied, ''Yes, except for a broken arm.''

''A broken arm, my God! What about Search and Rescue? Have they been alerted? They should be able to get him out of there quickly.''

''Yes, the Search and Rescue people have been notified and they're already on the move. There's only one problem.''

''What's that?''

''The crash area is covered in dense fog, and all indications are it won't move out for another twenty-four hours.''

''Good Lord! What about medical attention for the P.M.? Is his arm badly broken?''

''I don't know, Pierre. As you know, everything I get is second hand, maybe third. All I know is they're talking about parachuting in a doctor from the Canadian Airborne Regiment in Edmonton.''

''Into the fog? They must be out of their minds!''

The External Affairs Minister wanted to get off the line. He now had other things to do. ''Anyway, I thought Joe should know immediately. The press will probably be on to him in the next few minutes, as soon as they find out, because after all, Sands was coming to see him about this immigration thing."

"Right, Yves. I'll tell him immediately. Keep in touch." Pratte had no sooner put the telephone down when it rang again. Swinging his feet out of the bed to the floor, he picked up the telephone to be greeted by a loud voice at the other end. "Mr. Pratte, this is Oscar Bullit. I'm downstairs in the lobby. I left a message earlier but didn't get a reply. I've got to see the Prime Minister. I know he's all tied up, but this is critical. Can I come up?"

Pratte made the decision. The time set aside for the British Prime Minister had now opened up, and if Oscar Bullit said it was urgent, then it was urgent.

"Okay, Mr. Premier, but you've got to give him a half an hour. He's sleeping. You know we really came in straight from the Middle East, so he's exhausted. I have to get him up now anyhow. Can you give him half an hour, let's say twenty minutes? That should be enough."

Bullit accepted. "Yeah, that's fine. I'll grab a sandwich."

Pratte found the Prime Minister in his pyjamas busily shaving in the bathroom. When Roussel had digested the news about Sands' crash and was satisfied that rescue operations were underway, he returned to his shaving, talking over the hum of the electric razor.

"If the press call or want to come up and talk about the situation, I'll see them anytime. Any news about what's happening in England?"

"No, I haven't had a chance to find out anything." Pratte raised his voice to overcome the noise of the razor. "But Bullit's been after me. He wants to see you immediately, urgently. He's downstairs. I told him you would see him in about fifteen minutes from now."

The Prime Minister stopped his razor and turned to look at Pierre Pratte. "Bullit? What would he want? He hasn't had an urgent, let alone worthwhile, thought in his head since I've known him!"

"I haven't any idea, Joe, except that when Bullit says it's urgent, I believe it's urgent."

The Prime Minister went back to his shaving. "All right, I'll see him. He probably wants me to translate the message we sent him about the immigration policy from English into British Columbese."

"Now, now, Joe. Be kind," Pratte remonstrated.

The Prime Minister, with all the alcohol out of his system, moved briskly as he dressed, his mind working over the problems that would be created by Sands' plane crash. But the problems were really U.K. questions, not his. He wondered what that Cabinet at 10 Downing Street would be doing. The Chancellor of the Exchequer was in Washington, he knew that much. In Roussel's opinion, Hobson was much more a liability than an asset. Probably it was just as well he was in Washington so his staff bureaucrats could make the right decisions in his absence.

From the reports of the riots and gatherings across the country, the shutting of the banks, the country was clearly on the verge of anarchy. He shook his head. He never thought he'd live to see it. And the pressure to get people off those Islands. During the stopover at Ottawa, Parent had told him that by five Monday afternoon there was a queue of at least 5,000 people lined up at Canada House in London, waiting to make immigration applications. Today, Tuesday, that line would still be there, and even longer. Parent had asked Ontario and Alberta to make their offices in London available as alternative places where people could make application. Both governments had responded promptly. The Prime Minister guessed that as of today there would be line ups of 5,000 people at each of those places, too. Would his Cabinet refuse to take these people? He knew what he would do on the open-gate immigration question, but then, he was the Prime Minister. His intuition and instinct told him that on this question he should keep his own position to himself until he was forced. Sure, everyone would expect him as a French-Canadian to take the Quebec position, but let people guess.

He ran his comb through his straight black hair, which fell almost down to his collar, and then smoothed his black moustache. A fresh, dark grey vested suit had been put on the aircraft in Ottawa, along with a light blue shirt for the television cameras and a dark blue-and-white polka dot tie. With these on and his eyes showing only a slight trace of red, Prime Minister Roussel was ready for Oscar Bullit, or anyone else for that matter.

There was a tap on his bedroom door. It opened to show Pierre Pratte announcing Bullit's presence.

"Tell him I'll be there in a minute."

Roussel put the last finishing touches on his preparation for the rest of the day. It was doubtful if he would be able to have time to freshen up before the onslaught of people and meetings before dinner. As he entered the sitting room, he was heartily greeted by Oscar Bullit, a greeting which he returned in kind. The two of them were, after all, senior politicians, gentlemen, and even though they might hate each other's guts, they at least knew how to say hello cordially and in an apparently friendly way. Pratte excused himself, although he might just as well have been in the room because he could hear every word.

After being seated and declining the Prime Minister's offer of coffee, Bullit began.

"It's about the collapse of the U.K. economy and this business of people wanting to get off the Islands. The proposed open-gate immigration policy that the Brits want."

"Yes, the estimate is that we should plan to receive perhaps two million in the next year," the Prime Minister added.

"Right, Joe, I understand that. I've got my people really busting their bottoms to respond in time. When was it you wanted to have the information?"

"By tomorrow evening. Cabinet is meeting tomorrow night at eight to decide whether we'll accept the policy or not."

"Yeah, well, I just wanted to tell you myself that we out here in British Columbia, you know, we've got strong, strong ties with Great Britain, and we've got lots of land and lots of resources. Sure, it would be difficult to make adjustments to take a whole bunch of people all of a sudden. But we figure, I figure, that if a couple of million people have to get off those Islands, and it sure looks as though they're going to have to, well really, they're refugees, they've got to have someplace to go. We're prepared to take our fair share up here in this part of the world. I know your people down there in Ottawa don't really know anything about us and care less, but – "

Roussel laughed. "Come on now, Oscar. You're going to break that record one of these days."

Bullit laughed, too, but he was deadly serious about what he had said and about his attitude toward the east, and everything that the Prime Minister stood for.

He went on. "I decided I'd find out how somebody else thought about this situation, so I've been talking with your good friend and mine, the Premier of Alberta, Donald Purdy."

The mention of Purdy's name made the Prime Minister wince inwardly. Bullit continued.

"Strangely enough, he feels the same way I do. Out here in the west, we've got the land, the resources, and the job opportunities. We need people to balance off the enormous mass of humanity in central Canada, all you French-Canadians in Quebec and the great big Ontario industrial giant. Furthermore, both Purdy and I believe Canada has obligations to the Brits. They put this country together in the first place; they've given us a strong parliamentary system; we have close economic and cultural ties, and of course, we've got the Crown. Sure, the Queen is just a figurehead, but she is also a common bond. The monarchy is a common bond between us and Great Britain. Their Queen is our Queen, and through her and the monarchy and through the Commonwealth . . . Well, anyway, Purdy and I feel very strongly, and both our Cabinets are prepared to back us to the hilt.''

The Prime Minister could see nothing alarming about that statement. Is that why it was urgent that Bullit see him? ''I understand the position very well, Oscar, and I'm sure you will state it forcefully in your communication with us tomorrow.''

''Oh, yes, and I'll get after your two Cabinet ministers from out here, you can be sure of that.''

Roussel agreed. ''Yes, I'm sure you will.''

The Premier of British Columbia leaned forward, elbows on his knees, tense. ''We've just had word out here – it's on the radio and in the press – that Belisle has called a special meeting of the Quebec National Assembly tomorrow afternoon. He personally is going to propose a resolution that if the federal government adopts the open-gate immigration proposal, Quebec will secede. Have you heard about this, Joe?''

The Prime Minister shifted in his chair. ''Yes, I've heard about it.''

''And what are you going to do about it?''

The Prime Minister shrugged. ''What can I do about it? The Quebec National Assembly is entitled to pass whatever resolution or legislation it wishes on this point. I cannot dictate to them.''

Bullit pressed on. ''You mean to tell me that you're not going to do anything, either publicly or privately, to try to prevent them from passing such a resolution?''

"I've already talked to Gaston, tried to persuade him not to do this, but to this moment I haven't been successful."

"You realize, of course, that if Quebec goes out, your seat goes with it and your entire political base is destroyed. You're no longer the Prime Minister of Canada."

"Well, perhaps somebody in Ontario or the Maritimes will give up his seat for me."

"Prime Minister, you've got to be kidding! The only reason you're Prime Minister is because you've got Quebec."

Roussel threw up his right hand as if to wave off all this hypothetical speculation. "We'll see, we'll see. The government and the country will evolve as they should."

Bullit had arrived at the point which had brought him into Roussel's presence. "Let me put this into your evolutionary process. The Quebec National Assembly can make up its mind as to what it wants to do and by the same token, we can make up our minds out here in the west, what we want to do. I'm here to tell you, Prime Minister, that the governments of both Alberta and British Columbia and all members of both cabinets are 100 per cent together on this. Both B.C. and Alberta will secede from Confederation if the government of Canada refuses to adopt the open-gate immigration policy. We'll take them all ourselves!"

4:30 PM
Crash Site at Carr Lake
Near Baker Lake,
Northwest Territories
Canada

"I can hear them, sir!" Cranston exclaimed excitedly.

The distant rumble of aircraft engines was unmistakable. It was a Hercules Transport aircraft from 435 Squadron out of Edmonton, with a doctor from the Canadian Airborne Regiment on board. Squadron Leader Robins had been informed by Baker Lake about an hour earlier that the Herc was on its way, carrying the doctor who had volunteered to parachute in through the fog.

The Herc captain's voice came loud and clear through the VHF set. "RAF VC-10, this is Rescue 311. I am twenty miles south of your estimated position. Do you read me? Over."

Robins started to move toward the cockpit, but was halted momentarily by the Prime Minister, who had regained consciousness shortly after noon, but who was still weak and in pain. In addition to the effects of the broken arm, Sands had been badly upset by a difficult but brief conversation he had had with Acting P.M. Stanton, who had finally been able to get through to the Prime Minister shortly after one o'clock Baker Lake time, using the telephone/satellite/radio mix.

When Stanton told him that the Cabinet had decided for

166

martial law, Sands, even though under sedation, had reacted strongly. He was totally opposed to martial law. To him it was a total repudiation of Parliament and of democracy. It was another tragic error in a chain of disastrous choices. Sands had extracted from Stanton an undertaking that he would have Cabinet review the martial law resolution the next morning. Stanton would convey the Prime Minister's position, although he refused to give Sands a commitment that he would change his own position.

The Prime Minister clutched Robins' arm. "Basil, I don't want that doctor to jump. It's too risky. He won't be able to see the ground. There are rocks all over."

The squadron leader merely said, "Yes, sir." He walked quickly into the cockpit, picked up the microphone, and responded. "Rescue 311, Squadron Leader Robins here. We can hear you to the south. What's your plan of action?"

"Okay. We have Major LaFrance on board. He's the senior medical officer of the Canadian Airborne Regiment. He's also one of the top parachutists in the Canadian Armed Forces. I'll drop him from 1,300 feet. I've already checked the top of that fog and it's about 300. How thick is it on the ground?"

"Pea soup. You can barely see your hand in front of your face."

"That's what I thought. Okay, we're homing on your ELT* transmitter. When we hit the cone of silence directly above you, I'll proceed north for two minutes, then do a 180 to pass directly over you going southbound. Major LaFrance will jump when we hit the cone of silence again."

Robins was concerned. "That cone of silence can be fairly wide. If he jumps and misses us by much, he'll never find us. Can you hold for a few minutes. I may be able to organize a marker."

* Emergency Location Transmitter

"Sure, I can hold. I've got bags of fuel."

The squadron leader rushed into the lavatory at the front of the cabin next to the galley, at the same time shouting at Cranston. "Get two large pitchers out of the galley and fill them with kerosene. There should be some left in the starboard tanks."

In the lavatory Robins gathered up all the paper towels and toilet tissue he could lay his hands on. His arms filled with paper, he followed Cranston out the open cabin door on the port side, around to the rear of the broken aircraft, and back up the fuselage to the starboard wing. Cranston filled two huge pitchers with jet fuel from a fuel draincock. When the pitchers were filled and the draincock shut, the two men proceeded north through the clammy fog, picking their way carefully through a maze of small boulders. When he was satisfied that they were far enough away from the wreck, Robins stopped and threw the paper towels and toilet tissue on the ground, stacking it in a pile. He stood back as Cranston poured the two pitchers of jet fuel on the heap. Both of them moved back even further as the squadron leader struck a match and tossed it onto the mass of paper and kerosene. It immediately erupted into a ball of orange flame and thick black smoke, which quickly climbed straight up through the dense, almost windless fog.

High above them, circling to the north, the young Herc captain and his crew – all of them including the doctor were on the flight deck – anxiously scanned the brilliant white surface of the fog which blanketed the earth as far as the eye could see. It was hard to believe that down there, somewhere close by, on the flat, barren tundra, there was a huge, beautiful, broken bird and an injured Prime Minister of Great Britain.

Then he saw it: a thin column of black smoke piercing its way up through the solid, shimmering sunlit surface of the fog.

"I've got it. I've got it," shouted the smiling Herc pilot, pointing to the smoke.

Standing behind him on the flight deck, Doctor LaFrance nodded his head in satisfaction as his eyes found the black signal. That would make it much easier. Over the intercom the captain instructed his two loadmasters at the rear of the aircraft to open the main ramp under the tail and to prepare for the package drop. The medical equipment would be parachuted in first. With the smoke signal as a marker the doctor would be able to see exactly where the package and parachute entered the fog.

The major, fully dressed in military parachuting gear – protective helmet, jump boots, harness, and dark green jump suit – left the flight deck and climbed down to the floor of the huge cargo-carrying section of the Hercules. It was a confusion of uncovered bulkheads, pipes, wires, cables, and the special rolling tracks on the floor on which heavy cargo was moved on or off the aircraft. He reached down for his parachute lying on the collapsible canvas seats along the port side of the fuselage. The senior of the two loadmasters strapped his headset and microphone to his head and plugged into the communications box so he could hear the captain. He began lowering the ramp section of the fuselage, just below and slightly forward of the tail section. When in the closed position this hydraulically-operated ramp formed part of the fuselage and was of equal width. When it was lowered it came down to a flat position level with the floor of the cargo area.

By the time Major LaFrance had fastened on his chest safety chute, the ramp was fully lowered. The Hercules, uninsulated for sound, is a noisy aircraft at the best of times, but when the ramp is lowered in flight the combined noise of the four turboprop engines and the rushing air is deafening.

In accordance with the captain's instructions during the preflight briefing, the senior loadmaster would act as the

HERCULES

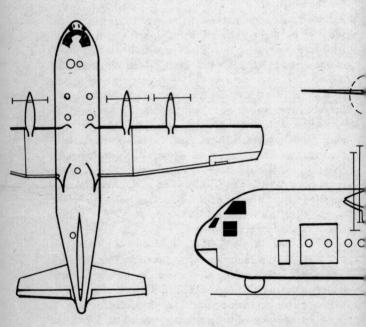

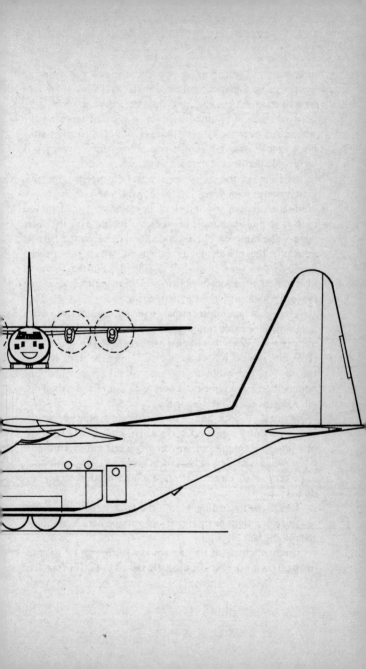

jumpmaster. The captain would give the order to drop the bundle as the Hercules went through the ELT's cone of silence by activating the green "jump" light near the ramp. Similarly, he would give the jump order for Major LaFrance on the second run over the target. However, with the clearly visible black smoke as a target, the opportunity for accuracy was increased and the captain's job was much easier.

As soon as the ramp door was fully opened the two loadmasters, with long safety straps hooked to harnesses around the upper parts of their bodies to prevent a fall, moved quickly to put the bundle of medical supplies near the outer edge of the ramp door. They did a final check on the harness attaching the bundle to its parachute, which was packed inside its own brown canvas bag. The flaps of the bag were held closed by a single pin, to which was attached a long lanyard with a catch hook at its opposite end.

The senior loadmaster attached the parachute lanyard to a long static line cable running along the ceiling of the fuselage, and tested it. When he and his partner shoved the bundle off the ramp, the catch hook would ride along the static wire on the roof of the cabin to the rear of the wire, where the parachute release pin would be pulled out of the parachute, allowing the parachute to open.

Major LaFrance had a similar lanyard attached to the locking pin on his main parachute. His chute was one of the new durable, high-accuracy, aerodynamically-controllable types, which enable a skilled parachutist to land consistently on a very small target. LaFrance would need accuracy this day.

He moved toward the rear of the aircraft, gave the senior loadmaster a thumbs-up signal and got one back in response. Everything was set to go.

On the flight deck, the captain was getting set for the run-in on target for the bundle drop. He talked to the loadmasters.

"I'm going to make the run-in steering about 180. I'll hold level at 600 feet, which should put us about 300 feet above the cloud or fog level. The lower I can get, the better. But the major has to be able to see the exact point where that bundle disappears in relation to the black smoke. It will go straight down. If he's going to find it on the ground in that dense crap, he's going to have to see it go into the fog."

"I'm now steering 360 and will be turning starboard for my run onto the target in two minutes. It is six minutes to the drop." The captain switched on the red jump warning light which shone brightly near the main ramp, a signal to the jumper and loadmasters to be ready.

The loadmaster acknowledged, "Six minutes to the drop, sir. Ramp door is open and secure. Bundle and parachute in position and attached to static line."

The captain eased back on the power. With the ramp down he was flying at 150 knots and thirty degrees of flap. He would now reduce speed for the run to 130 knots. He eased the Hercules into a gentle turn to starboard and, as his air speed reduced to the drop speed of 130 knots, he put down fifty degrees of flap. By the time he had completed his turn for the final run-in on the target, the column of black smoke piercing the brilliant white sun-bathed fog blanket stood out clearly. The aircraft was flying steadily at drop speed, 130 knots, at 600 feet above sea level.

"One minute to drop," came the pilot's warning, which was immediately acknowledged by the senior loadmaster. The captain calculated he would have to get the bundle out about one second before the aircraft hit the black smoke which was now very close.

"Fifteen seconds to drop."

Again there was an immediate acknowledgement. The two loadmasters were in position on each side of the bundle, hands in position on it, ready to shove it out on the captain's "go" signal. Both of them stared at the green light, waiting for the instant it was illuminated.

They were coming up fast to the column of black smoke. Everything was set.

The captain fingered the green light switch. At the precise moment he flicked it on.

At the rear of the aircraft, the green signal flashed. The two crewmen heaved mightily on the bundle. With its parachute it shot out into the slipstream. The static line strap ripped the pin from the parachute container from which the red parachute canopy quickly streamed, twisting, then burst open to begin its descent with its precious cargo. A split second after the parachute began to billow from its container, LaFrance caught sight of black smoke swirling by and for an instant he could detect the acrid smell of burning kerosene.

The senior loadmaster reported to the pilot, "Bundle away, sir. Parachute opened okay. Static line in and secure."

"Good. How did we do?"

"Perfect, sir. The chute's just entered the clag, about fifty feet south of the smoke column."

LaFrance had not taken his eyes off the parachute from the instant it opened. As it disappeared into the fog, he had its precise position buttoned down.

The captain reported to Robins, who was waiting in the cockpit of the crashed VC-10. "The bundle's away. Right on the button. It should be about fifty feet south of the fire. I'm just turning north again to get set up for the run-in for the major's jump."

Robins' voice came back. "Jolly good. And remember, get him to come down north of the smoke, not south. Our aircraft is to the south of the smoke. I don't want him to land on us."

"Wilco, sir." Back to the intercom: "Six minutes!" the captain warned. In the cabin the red warning light went on and the green was extinguished. "I'm turning starboard now to head back north for the run-in for the major's jump. We'll use the same procedures except I'll be at 1,300 feet so he can have 1,000 in which to get himself organized before he hits the fog. Tell him to go in just to the north of the smoke, not, repeat, not, to the south of it."

Again the captain put the Herc through a gentle 180° turn to the north, climbing at the same time to 1,300 feet, thirty degrees of flaps down, 150 knots. Then he turned south toward the still present but dispersing black smoke.

"One minute to jump," the captain alerted the loadmasters, who acknowledged.

On the ramp at the rear of the aircraft, the senior loadmaster shouted into LaFrance's ear, "Remember, land to the north of the smoke. One minute to jump." He held up his left hand with the index finger indicating one. LaFrance nodded in acknowledgement. He was ready.

The lanyard from his parachute to the static line was fastened for automatic opening when he jumped. LaFrance had over two hundred jumps to his credit and normally was not nervous, but this time he was tense because of the high risk. He had never heard of anybody who had jumped into dense fog, hurtling down to hit the ground blind in terrain strewn with treacherous boulders. It would be stupid to have him wind up with a broken leg or arm, a casualty himself. But it was a chance which had to be taken.

The captain's voice barked over the intercom, "Fifteen seconds to jump." The senior loadmaster acknowledged, then held his left hand up toward LaFrance, palm out, fingers widespread; then he retracted his fingers into a clenched fist three times, the visual fifteen-second signal. LaFrance nodded. He was poised, crouched at the edge of the ramp. The loadmaster stood to his right and slightly behind, steadying himself by gripping the bar of the retracted canvas seat. All eyes were glued on the green glass.

Suddenly it burst into light.

The loadmaster slapped LaFrance on the shoulder, shouting "Go!" at the top of his lungs. LaFrance reacted instantly, leaping unhesitatingly into the air, using his arms and legs to correct the tendency to tumble on hitting the slipstream. The lanyard attached to the static line slapped against the butt end of its travel and the holding pin came cleanly out of the flaps of the containing bag. Immediately the bright red parachute began to stream from it. As the chute opened, LaFrance's body absorbed the abrupt impact of the sudden slash in speed. Then he was swinging under the chute in a gentle, pendulum arc.

He could see he had been perfectly positioned by the Herc captain. The parachute had opened directly over the black smoke column below. He pulled on his left control cord and began a gentle turn in that direction, circling gradually as he approached the surface of the fog. At the instant of entry he should have as little forward or backward speed as possible. He wanted to be going absolutely straight down. His descent rate of twelve feet per second would take him through 250 feet of fog in about twenty-five seconds.

Continuing to circle slowly, eyes on the smoke marker, he looked up for a moment at the Hercules moving away from him to the south. He knew the crew would be watching his descent and would be anxiously awaiting a report from the ground. The fog was coming up fast. LaFrance stopped the circling directly above the desired point of entry, facing east, just north of the smoke which he could now smell clearly.

Then he was in it: thick, heavy fog totally engulfed him. It was like being suspended in a vacuum. No sense of movement, no sound except for the distant drone of the Hercules, nothing. The cords from his body to his parachute disappeared a foot above his head.

"A thousand and six, a thousand and seven, a thousand

and eight." His mind kept up the count of seconds. Suddenly the eerie silence was pierced by a sharp, high-pitched sound from beneath him and to his right. Startled, it took him a split second to realize it was a whistle. Someone was blowing a whistle. Then the whistle was joined by the sound of hard banging on metal. Both sounds came from the same source, below and to his right.

Still counting the seconds, his mouth moved as he silently recited the numbers. He lifted his right arm stiffly, pointing toward the spot the sound was coming from. That would be the location of the VC-10. He knew he was well to the north of it, perhaps 125 yards. If his right arm kept monitoring the position of the whistling and pounding, it would provide another way other than counting to check his position above the ground.

"A thousand and ten, a thousand and eleven." Halfway down. His right arm was about forty-five degrees from the vertical line of his body.

At the count of eighteen seconds, LaFrance's right arm was pointing close to the horizontal. He was almost at the ground. In came his right arm as his body automatically took up the landing position, knees slightly bent to allow the muscles to take the shock, arms high on the shroud lines.

"Anytime now, anytime now," he told himself as he stared straight down, hoping to get a split second glimpse of the ground before hitting it.

He saw the tundra as he hit. The force of the blind impact shocked him physically and mentally. He was expecting it, but he was not totally ready for it. His superbly conditioned, trained body responded perfectly, the leg muscles absorbing his heavy weight as he hit. He staggered backward slightly. His left heel caught on a small boulder, throwing him heavily backwards to the ground. During the instant of the fall, he could see the red canopy of the parachute settling down upon him. When he landed on his back the wind was knocked out of him. His head hit another boulder. But it was a glancing blow which his protective helmet easily withstood.

Lying flat out, attempting to regain his breath, LaFrance knew he had sustained no injuries. A stroke of luck. He waited for a few seconds before attempting to move. The fabric of the parachute had covered his face, filling his blinking eyes with its red colour as the murky light inside the fog penetrated the thin, nylon material. To his right, the banging and whistling continued.

The major sat up and unhooked the parachute harness from his body, pulling the canopy material toward him until he found the edge, which he threw back over his shoulders. Then he was clear.

Standing up, he turned toward the source of the sound and shouted, "It's okay. I'm down."

Instantly the noise stopped.

A strong English voice called, "Are you all right, major?"

"Yeah, had the wind knocked out of me, but I'm okay. If you'll do the whistling and banging bit again, I'll come to the aircraft. Will someone let the Herc know I'm all right?"

Leaving the parachute, his senses monitoring the location of the sound, LaFrance slowly made his way to Robins' whistle and Cranston's banging on the fuselage. The fog was so thick that he was only four feet away from them when he emerged. His wraithlike appearance in front of them startled both men for an instant. The banging and whistling gave way to handshaking and warm greeting.

After taking a quick look at the Prime Minister without taking off the splint, LaFrance went out again into the fog in search of his much needed bundle of medical supplies. Cranston went with him. First they found the remains of the fire, but not without some difficulty. From there they headed south toward the aircraft where Robins was again using his whistle intermittently to give them a marker. LaFrance held Cranston's left hand with his right so they would not be separated. Before they found the precious bundle, they had made two search attempts, each time moving out about fifty feet from the fire location.

Before removing the splint to treat the haggard, suffering Prime Minister, the doctor gave him an injection which knocked him out again. It was just as well. LaFrance found that he had to reset the bone. This done and fresh splints applied, the doctor checked Sands' heart and blood pressure. Both were satisfactory, although the blood pressure was a bit higher than he would like to have seen it.

His ministrations to the Prime Minister completed for the moment, LaFrance went to his medical supply bundle, which had been placed on the floor by the cabin door. With a smile on his face, he announced to the conscious survivors of the crash, "Gentlemen, I have brought a special gift for each of you."

He bent over, reached in, and pulled out four cans of insect repellent, to the sounds of shouts of gratitude.

"And one bottle of Cognac and two of Scotch!"

The shouts became cheers.

8:05 PM
The Cabinet Room of the White House
Washington, D.C.

In the White House Cabinet Room, Secretary of State Jessica Swift sat in the chair immediately to the right of the President's. He was in the Oval Office and would join them later. On her right was the Secretary of the Treasury, Herman Schwartz, the brilliant Los Angeles banker. To the left of the President's chair was the Secretary of Labor, Lincoln Hamilton of Detroit, the first black American to have that post. None of them had staff present, an indication that this would be an exploratory meeting only. This trio, specially selected and appointed by the President from among the best brains in the United States, faced the Chancellor of the Exchequer, Michael Hobson.

Member of Parliament for the riding of Ashford in Kent, the proprietor of a wine importing firm in London – it had been in the family for seventy years – Hobson had had to learn French fluently as a young man entering the business. At the time of his appointment as Chancellor of the Exchequer the critics noted his lack of experience and background for the post. Nevertheless, inexperienced and untrained as he was in fiscal and monetary matters, Hobson had learned very quickly and bilingualism had helped. He was a hard worker, intelligent, with a near-photographic memory. And since

180

British Cabinet members are selected from among the elected members of the party in power, the holder of a ministerial portfolio need not bring to the job any prior knowledge or experience in the areas of his particular responsibility. Therefore, enormous responsibility is placed upon the civil servants, the deputy ministers and the deputy secretaries, the people who head the bureaucracy. They stay at the top of the departmental pinnacle while ministers come and go. Over the years, it is the civil servants who have provided the solid base and the expertise for the politicians to draw upon.

Unfortunately for Hobson, the nature of the British collapse had released a torrent of economic problems which prevented him from bringing with him the senior mandarin, the Chief Secretary of the Treasury. It was absolutely essential that somebody "mind the shop." Hobson's elected parliamentary secretary, who was his assistant in the House of Commons, together with the chief secretaries and a group of assistant deputy ministers, would perform the crucial task of advising the Cabinet.

Hobson had a full report on the resignation of the Governor of the Bank of England. Dreadful fellow anyhow, in the Chancellor's view, and good riddance. On the other hand, Hobson knew he would be severely taken to task when he and the Prime Minister next met. And, of course, he knew that he was partly at fault in getting his advice from the Deputy Governor of the Bank, who had no knowledge of the Governor's arrangements for interim emergency financing should a crisis arise. If Hobson had known of the contingency plans, he would have advised the Cabinet to keep the banks open, while freezing Arab deposits. Instead, the collapse of the British economy was certified.

But the Chancellor refused to accept any blame. He had contacted the Deputy Governor and sought his advice; if the Governor had failed to communicate to the Deputy Governor what he was doing, then it was the Governor's fault, not Hobson's, and it was proper that the Governor should resign. In any event, that would be Hobson's argument when he was called to account. He was still Chancellor of the Exchequer, and until such time as the Prime Minister chose to remove him, he would remain so.

During his wait in Washington, he had completed negotiations with the IMF for the five billion dollars which the former Governor of the Bank of England had arranged. The IMF people would not go higher until they knew what the United States was going to do. Also he had kept in constant touch with the Chief Secretary and with members of the Cabinet, particularly with Acting Prime Minister Stanton. It was obvious to him that they were getting most of their advice from the Chief Secretary of the Treasury, but at least they had the courtesy to check with the Chancellor on some of the more important matters as they came up. Of course, if he had known the President was going to insist on waiting until the Secretary of State arrived back in Washington before meeting with him, the Chancellor would have remained in London until it was certain when the Secretary would be arriving.

On the advice of the Chief Secretary, he had brought along with him two people: an assistant deputy minister, a young man who had an excellent understanding of the world banking system and the funds available for emergency use; and another man, the Chancellor's executive assistant. Both men accompanied him to this meeting, the assistant deputy sitting on his right and the executive assistant on his left, as the three powerful Secretaries, State, Labor, and Treasury, opened this crucial meeting.

Jessica Swift took immediate command. She was the senior Secretary and as such her colleagues, and indeed the Chancellor, automatically deferred to her. She advised the group of her meeting with the King of Saudi Arabia, but cautioned the Chancellor that under no circumstances should he be optimistic about the possibility of her having convinced the King to reverse his course of action.

"As I advised the President – and I could not inform your government of the meeting or its results until I had reported to the President, which I did a few minutes ago – the major difficulty for the King would be a loss of face should he reverse his decision. Anyway, the effort has been made, Mr. Chancellor, and if we succeed, we succeed. If we do not, we do not."

"Well Madam Secretary," Hobson added, "if there is anyone in the world who could have changed his mind, you're that person."

She responded without smiling. "Thank you. Occasional flattery, well deserved or not, helps to sustain the spirit."

"Now let's get down to business. First, let me apologize on the President's behalf for the delay in meeting with you. I hope he will be along shortly, even if only for a few minutes, but the President felt it was absolutely essential that all three of us, Labor, Treasury, and State, meet with you."

Hobson nodded silently.

"On the other hand," Secretary Swift continued, "this delay has given our respective staffs a chance to do a great deal of preliminary work."

The Chancellor broke in. "Yes, as a matter of fact, I've been talking with people in all three of your departments. I have given them a list of the items for discussion, an agenda if you will, of the crucial items that we need your help on."

The Secretary of State nodded. "Yes, we've seen that. All of us have copies. Perhaps we could just discuss this list briefly. Then we can begin to deal with it at length. By the way, Mr. Hobson, I think we should look at this meeting as being preliminary only. I don't think we can settle anything tonight, and furthermore, I'd like to have a full staff briefing tomorrow morning for my own people, as well as Treasury and Labor."

Both her colleagues nodded in agreement. "And I think we should meet again tomorrow afternoon when I'm sure we can finalize matters."

"But Dr. Swift," the Chancellor objected, "time is of the essence. We've already lost a day, and now to suggest that we will meet tomorrow afternoon . . . As you know, I'm the Chancellor. I really should be in England. I should be at Cabinet. I should be there, not here."

Her reply was calm but cutting. "And I suppose it follows that your Prime Minister should be there, in London, instead of in a crashed aircraft in the middle of nowhere. No, it seems to me that if Britain is going to be bailed out of this mess, the decisions that are going to do it are going to be taken right here, in this room, within the next twenty-four hours." She was trying to be gentle. "So it seems to me that while it may be difficult for you, you must be patient with us while we try to assess the implications of your request for monetary support, to assess the future prospects of your monetary situation, and to determine whether your country can turn itself around. You know, you're asking the United States to make enormous commitments, not only in terms of money, but people as well. This open-gate immigration policy – we just can't snap our fingers and say, 'Sure, let them come.' Nor by the same token can we snap our fingers and say, 'No, they can't come.' All of these matters are locked together. If we lend you twenty-five billion dollars, what are the prospects for repayment, or even a payment of interest? And if we guarantee your loans from the International Monetary Fund or any other fund, what happens if you default? And is it essential to the restoration of your economy that people get off the Islands en masse? And if so, what's the impact on us? We're just not about to advise the President to go any faster, Mr. Chancellor."

Hobson looked uncomfortable. "I suppose you're right.

It's just that I feel rather out of things, out of touch, and I want to get back as quickly as I can."

The Secretary of Labor, a short, round-faced, tough man, joined in with a forceful, low voice. "We understand your anxiety, Mr. Hobson, but I've got to agree with Dr. Swift. So why don't we get on with this agenda."

They did. They dealt with direct loans from the United States and loans from the International Monetary Fund (an additional $5 billion) and the OECD fund ($5 billion); the future supply of crude oil to the U.K. and the financing of that supply; and the final item, the proposed open-gate immigration policy.

Midway through the meeting, which concluded shortly before 11:00 PM, the President briefly joined them with news that the Prime Minister had not yet been rescued, and that it was likely the fog wouldn't lift until the next day around noon.

The President asked Hobson, "Have you talked with him yet?"

"No, I haven't, sir."

"Well you should. The Baker Lake radio operator can hook you in by telephone and radio."

"Yes, well, I thought I might wait until after this meeting, and have a word with him then."

"I assume you've got clearance from him on the points you're raising with us."

"Yes, of course." Not totally true, but why erode his credibility with these people. Anything they agreed upon he would have to have confirmed by the Cabinet in any event. Besides, he knew what had to be done.

The President was in a hurry. He had the fullest confidence in his three Cabinet members and agreed with their proposal to have their staff briefings in the morning and then have a negotiating session beginning in early afternoon. That suited him fine. He would clear the afternoon so he could take full part in the discussions.

Just before he got up to leave, the President said to the Chancellor, "You know, you people are asking us for a lot, in fact, an incredible amount of support. You're going to have to face up to the fact that if we agree to go along with you, there will have to be certain terms and conditions you'll have to live up to, that we'll demand from you."

Hobson unhesitatingly agreed. "Certainly, Mr. President. I have no idea what you have in mind . . ."

"Try this one on for size," the President responded. "One of the keys to your economic future – revival, survival, whatever you want to call it – your way out of bankruptcy, is to get the North Sea crude oil onshore and become self-sufficient as quickly as possible. Right?"

"No question about that."

"Okay. Now this isn't a condition, but I want you to think about this question: How would the U.K. government guarantee that the British trade unions will be barred from – prohibited from being involved in any way, either directly or indirectly – participating in the development of the North Sea crude oil fields, or the building of the ships or equipment, or the floating drilling rigs, pipelines, and refineries to handle the North Sea development?"

The Chancellor of the Exchequer looked shocked. "That can't be done. Why, that's impossible, Mr. President. The unions wouldn't stand for it!"

The President was emphatic. "It seems to me that we're soon going to find out who's running the United Kingdom, the trade unions or the government, because I can tell you one thing for sure, and it's this: before the United States puts one red cent behind you people, we're going to have to be satisfied there will be a crash program – and I mean crash, just like the Manhattan project in World War II when we put the atomic bomb together – a crash program to get you people self-sufficient, to get your crude oil onshore." He stood up, still talking. The others respectfully stood up with him. "So between the time you finish this meeting and our meeting tomorrow afternoon, I suggest you consult with your Cabinet colleagues and come up with a proposal which will satisfy us that you're going to do a crash North Sea program. One of the pieces of that plan will have to deal with the union question."

Again Hobson protested. "Surely, Mr. President, you can't expect me or my Cabinet in a period of just a few hours to come up with such a plan?"

"But just a little while ago you were complaining that the time between now and tomorrow afternoon was far too long," the Secretary of State remarked.

"Well, this is different," Hobson replied.

The President reached across the table to shake Hobson's hand in departure, saying, with a smile, the smile of an astute politician, "You can do it, Mr. Chancellor. But if you don't come up with a plan, I will."

Wednesday, July 7

12:00 NOON
Crash Site at Carr Lake
Near Baker Lake,
Northwest Territories
Canada

The Prime Minister of the United Kingdom, Jeremy Sands, looked at his watch now strapped to his right wrist. He shook his head in frustration and disgust. Here he was, trapped in the middle of nowhere, fogged in, with no immediate prospect of getting out, while crucial decisions were being made at one of the most critical times in his country's long history.

From the time of LaFrance's jump late the previous day until now, there had been little contact with the outside world, even though the communication line was open through the Baker Lake radio station. Basil Robins had decided that in order to conserve the power in the batteries, the VHF radio should be switched on only on the half-hour and the hour, and then only until all necessary messages and conversations were completed.

Sands had regained consciousness about half an hour after the doctor had reset his broken arm. He quickly regained most of his strength after a meal of emergency rations and a healthy shot of Scotch and water. During the evening he had talked with the President of the United States at length, although it was not possible to delve into any sensitive areas when all the

191

world was able to listen. The Secretary of State had arrived back at Washington; she and the President were about to meet with the Chancellor of the Exchequer and his people. If they needed to consult with the Prime Minister, they would contact him on the hour or half-hour. To add to the Prime Minister's frustration and concern, no such call had come, not even a status report from Hobson.

However, he had talked with Acting Prime Minister Stanton. His call had come through on the eight o'clock sequence that morning, which was three in the afternoon at 10 Downing Street. The Cabinet had confirmed the decision to keep the banks closed until noon on Thursday, July 8, pending the outcome of the discussions in Washington. Stanton hadn't had a report from Hobson either, or any request for guidance, although Hobson had talked with the Acting Governor of the Bank of England on three occasions Stanton knew of. The good news was that Cabinet had lifted the martial law edict, a move which had been well received by the people and the press. This action relieved a mounting hostile confrontation with the increasingly rebellious unemployed.

Stanton informed Sands that the pound had gone up to $1.10 U.S. at the opening of European trading that morning, but had fallen back to $1.05. The emigration queues at the American, Canadian, Australian, and New Zealand offices were blocks long. Emergency offices would be opened as soon as positive responses to the open-gate emigration proposals had come from the four English-language countries – if they came at all.

The Shah of Iran was prepared to see the Prime Minister anytime, and had called Stanton personally to assure him that Iran would continue its supply of crude oil to the U.K., with an increase of 25 per cent. That was all the Shah could allocate at that time. The financing for the continued supply would be worked out once the U.K.'s negotiations for funding had been settled, however long that might take.

The final message from Stanton was that Thomas Short, Leader of the Opposition, had advised Stanton that he was prepared to negotiate for a National Government as soon as the Prime Minister got back to London. However, Tom Short insisted that Parliament be recalled not later than Monday next. The Prime Minister agreed that this should be done. From the barren Arctic tundra near Baker Lake, Northwest Territories, Canada, came the instruction that an emergency session of the Parliament of the United Kingdom should be called.

At twelve noon on Wednesday July 7, Squadron Leader Robins switched on the VHF radio and called Baker Lake for messages.

"The first message is about the weather," the Baker Lake operator replied. "It's looking good. We think the fog will begin to disperse in about two or three hours, maybe four."

Robins received this news enthusiastically. "Excellent! Have the Search and Rescue people passed any messages about their plans for getting us out of here?"

"Yes," Baker Lake responded. "I have just been talking with the searchmaster. He's at Churchill with two Voyageur helicopters, the big ones, but they're weathered in at this time with fog and rain. He expects the soonest they can get out of Churchill will probably be six to eight hours from now."

The squadron leader's optimism quickly faded. "And I suppose it'll take the choppers at least three hours to get here."

"I don't know, sir. I think you should talk to the searchmaster at Churchill directly. Stand by one and I'll see if I can raise him by telephone."

In a short time Baker Lake was back. "VC-10, I have the searchmaster, Captain Partridge, on the line. Go ahead."

"Captain Partridge, Robins here. It looks as though the fog will be clearing very shortly, but I understand you're weathered in. Can you tell me what your plans are, please?"

Robins could hear the captain's voice clearly through the telephone link. "Will do, sir. I am at Churchill, about 350 miles south of your position. We have a stationary trough at this time. It's producing fog and rain, and has weathered my choppers in. Looks as though we won't be clear for at least six to eight hours. When we did get going, we'd have to refuel at Eskimo Point on the way up. So I estimate that, from the time of departure from Churchill, we'd have to add another five hours before we're able to lift you out. But I have an alternative plan which may get you out faster."

Robins' face brightened. "Shoot," he replied instantly.

"Right. There are two single engine STOL* Air Reserve Otters located at Coral Harbour on Southampton Island. They're working with a government survey crew. They've got balloon tires and litters for medical evacuation. Their crews are highly competent, experienced Arctic people. My plan is to put them in to get you. All you have to do when the fog clears is find an esker – a long bed of gravel, could be miles long, twenty to thirty feet wide. Find an esker, then pick out a stretch on it, preferably about 1,000 feet long. Make sure it's clear of boulders or large stones. Mark the ends in some way."

Major LaFrance, who was standing in the cockpit with Robins listening to the conversation, interjected. "We'll use my parachutes. They're both red. We can put one at each end." Robins nodded in agreement as the searchmaster went on.

"You'll be able to talk with the Otters on the Baker Lake frequency to give them landing instructions. They have your exact position. I've already moved the Otters from Coral

*STOL: Short Take-Off and Landing

Harbour to the airstrip at Chesterfield Inlet, which is now clear of fog. That puts them about ninety nautical miles from your location. It will take them one hour to reach your position. Assuming the forecast is right, and God knows if it is, your fog should begin to clear about four hours from now, which is sixteen hundred hours local time. So I'll launch the Otters out of Chesterfield Inlet at fifteen hundred hours. They'll be overhead at sixteen hundred. They'll have seven hours of fuel onboard when they leave Chesterfield. In the event your fog doesn't clear, I can let them hold over your position for three hours and fifteen minutes before they have to break off. Assuming they get in, they'll lift your party direct to Baker Lake to be picked up by the Herc aircraft which will be standing by. If the Herc can't get into Baker Lake, we'll put it into either Chesterfield, Rankin, or Eskimo Point; but I'll advise. I suggest that after fifteen hundred hours you leave your VHF set on to monitor any messages that I want to pass."

Everyone on the downed VC-10 had heard the conversation and all were again optimistic. From the cockpit Squadron Leader Robins could see the smiling face of the injured Prime Minister who was sitting up in his cabin seat. Sands gave a thumbs-up signal as Robins said to the searchmaster, "Good show, captain. You're damned well organized and that's comforting. We've read your message loud and clear. We'll get to work on the landing strip as soon as we have some visibility here. We'll leave our radio on after fifteen hundred hours."

There were only four vacant member's seats out of 110 in the Quebec National Assembly. The galleries were jampacked. After the formalities for the opening of the special session were completed, the atmosphere was tense and expectant as the Premier of Quebec stood up to speak.

All eyes focused on the tall, spare, sixty-two-year-old Gaston Belisle as he rose to his feet. His was an ominous figure, dressed in a black suit, his long, sharp-featured face topped by a thick head of jet black hair, notwithstanding his age. Even his horn-rimmed glasses were black. This powerful political leader had had his problems in recent months in spite of the enormous majority he carried in the Assembly. His difficulties had been brought on by scandals of various kinds within the development industry of the province. Unfortunately for him, they had reached right into his government. He had fought hard for his credibility, desperately searching for an issue which would enable him to entice the people of Quebec to forget about the problems of the past and stand behind him for the future.

He now had that issue, behind which he was certain all

196

Quebec would unite, including the opposition parties in the legislature.

The Premier looked around the silent chamber. Then he began.

"Mr. Speaker, this day and this hour are the most important in the entire history of the Quebec National Assembly and all the legislatures which preceded it from the time of the British Conquest on the Plains of Abraham. For it is on this day, in this hour, that notice will be served upon the government of Canada and upon the people of Canada that Quebec stands ready to leave Confederation.

"In the past, we have fought hard, Quebec has fought hard, to preserve our language, our culture, our French-Canadian way of life against the constant, unending encroachments of *les anglais*. The threat of domination by the English language we have attempted to counter by the enactment of Bill 22, which has established French as the official language of Quebec. This legislation, while controversial, has been a dramatic step forward in the protection of our cultural sovereignty. No longer will *Québecois* have to suffer the humiliating requirement that they must speak English in order to obtain employment or to achieve advancement in the factories and industries which populate this province.

"Unfortunately, a very large proportion, indeed an overwhelming proportion of those same factories and industries are owned by English-Canadians or by Americans, who see Quebec as nothing more than an economic colony, and who until now have expected to do business here using the English language.

"This government is dedicated to the dominance of the French language and the French-Canadian culture within the boundaries of this French-Canadian state. For, Mr. Speaker, Quebec truly is a state onto itself, more clearly established than any other on this continent. We have our territory clearly defined. We have this powerful National Assembly, totally capable of self-government for Quebec. Among the majority of our people we have a single, common, powerful religion. We have a common, unique language, and we have a common culture, almost all of us having descended from the very small group of intelligent, resourceful, capable French people who lived here at the time of the Conquest. If you put all of these ingredients together, Mr. Speaker, you have the stuff of which independence, sovereignty, and self-determination are made.

"In the past two decades, this government and those which preceded it have caused studies to be carried out on the question of whether Quebec would be an economically viable unit in the event of its separation from Canada. These studies have shown conclusively that Quebec could survive, and indeed, prosper. Furthermore, I have said in the past and say again today that I believe we can have a politically independent French Quebec in North America within an economic common market with Canada. Should the resolution which I propose to place before this legislature, Mr. Speaker, be implemented, then one of the basic objectives would be not only independence and sovereignty for Quebec, but as well an economic common market with Canada.

"Another source of Quebec's strength is, of course, France, our original mother nation. She is now taking a renewed interest in Quebec's economic development, particularly in the field of mineral resources and in the transformation of our transport and telecommunications systems. I am certain that France will at all times be available to us for guidance and assistance should we call upon that great nation. You will recall, Mr. Speaker, that President Valery Giscard d'Estaing has said to all *Québecois,* 'I remember, and I shall remember.'

"Now, Mr. Speaker, let me turn to the crucial issue which brings us here today. The economy of the United Kingdom is in total collapse. The value of the pound has been cut in half in relation to other currencies. Unemployment in Britain is almost at the three million mark and rising, with factories being shut down everywhere. Food shortages are imminent. The Arabs are withdrawing their investments from the United Kingdom and have cut off their oil supplies. In the face of this calamity, the British government has adopted an open-gate emigration policy and has asked Canada, the United States, Australia, and New Zealand to reciprocate by creating comparable policies, so that those who leave the United Kingdom can go to the country of their choice. It is estimated that the total exodus off the Islands will be in the neighbourhood of 10 per cent of the population, that is, between five and one-half and six million people. It is also estimated that approximately two million of those would elect to come to Canada."

There was no sign of emotion among his audience as the Premier spoke. In the last two days everyone had learned through the news media the facts he was stating.

"Of this number, probably none would come to the province of Quebec. They would go to English Canada, probably Toronto, Winnipeg, Edmonton, and Vancouver, and perhaps a few to the Maritimes. And they would all come, that is to say, almost all, within the next year, as food shortages and unemployment, coupled with unstoppable inflation of over 50 per cent in the past two years, force people to leave.

"Unfortunately, Mr. Speaker, this massive inflow of people into Canada would almost overnight reduce the percentage of Quebec's share of Canada's total population from the present 28 per cent to 25.6 per cent, assuming an influx of two million people. On this basis, Quebec would lose between six and seven of its seventy-four seats in the House of Commons."

There were gasps of surprise from the gallery.

"Just think how much easier it would be for English-Canadians to form a majority government in Ottawa without Quebec. The bargaining position of Quebec's members of the House of Commons and the Québecois Cabinet ministers in Ottawa would be seriously weakened, as indeed would the position of the government of Quebec in its dealings with the federal government and the rest of Canada. The opportunity to conserve special constitutional privileges for Quebec as the home of French culture in Canada would be diminished. Without question, the official federal policy of bilingualism across Canada would be put aside.

"What is all the more shocking, Mr. Speaker, is that even without massive British immigration to Canada within the next year, a study of population trends in Canada to the year 2001, which was released by Statistics Canada in June of 1974, shows that Quebec's share of the total population of Canada could shrink from the present 28 per cent to 22.6 per cent by the year 2001. This would reduce Quebec's number of seats in the House of Commons to sixty out of 264, compared with Quebec's present seventy-four seats. Now if you further reduce the number of seats by seven through a massive British influx, the potential is that by the year 2001, Quebec would be entitled to only fifty-three seats in the House of Commons. In a word, Quebec, French Canada, would be swamped by English Canada."

Again a rise of muttering through the chamber.

"For all of these reasons, Mr. Speaker, I have informed the Prime Minister of Canada, himself a French-Canadian and a son of Quebec, that Quebec cannot withstand the harmful results of a massive influx of English-speaking British citizens under an open-gate immigration policy."

His words were greeted by desk-thumping applause from all members of the legislature, and unprecedented and

200

normally unacceptable applause and whistling from the gallery. When it subsided, the Premier continued.

"French-Canadians are by their nature a family-oriented, humane, kind people. Under normal circumstances, they would be the first to offer succour to any suffering nation. The offering to Great Britain of food and economic aid to the limit and beyond would be a policy of the federal government which Quebec would support without hesitation or reservation, even if it meant great sacrifices for our people. But the sudden movement of two million Britons into English Canada would strike a death blow to Quebec, to our unique language and culture. It is totally unacceptable."

More vigorous applause. The Premier remained sober-faced, unsmiling.

"Mr. Speaker, the federal Cabinet meets tonight to consider the question of whether or not to accept the open-gate immigration policy. The press has widely reported that British Columbia and Alberta have informed the federal government that if the open-gate policy is not accepted, they will secede from Confederation and themselves adopt an open-gate policy. The removal of Alberta and its enormous energy resources from Confederation would be a serious blow to the rest of Canada. I have no doubt, knowing the two strong leaders of both those provinces, that they would immediately move to secede should the decision go against them. It follows that should the resolution I will now present to the Assembly be carried, the federal government will be in an unparalleled dilemma.

"Be that as it may, Mr. Speaker, I move the following resolution, which will be seconded by the Leader of the Opposition:

"RESOLVED that the National Assembly of Quebec is opposed to the creation by the federal government of any

201

changes to the current immigration legislation and regulations of Canada in order to create special immigration privileges for citizens of the United Kingdom; and more particularly, is opposed to the establishment of an open-gate immigration policy whereby as many Britons who elect to come to Canada may do so; and that in the event the federal government does so create special immigration privileges or adopts the aforesaid open-gate immigration policy, then Quebec shall forthwith secede from Canada and the government of Quebec will by this resolution be instructed to take all steps immediately and do all things necessary to effect secession, including the bringing of the appropriate legislation before the National Assembly."

The chamber erupted in a standing ovation which went on for several minutes. There was no debate. There was no need.

The emergency session of the Quebec National Assembly was adjourned when the clerk had finished the recorded vote. It was unanimous.

3:12 PM
Crash Site at Carr Lake,
Northwest Territories
Canada

At twelve minutes past three, Cranston, standing at the port
entrance door, exclaimed, "Look, it's lifting!" as he pointed
outside. All except the Prime Minister rushed to windows on
each side of the aircraft.

"You're right," Robins shouted from the cockpit. Mag-
ically, they could suddenly see a hundred, perhaps 200 yards
from the aircraft. LaFrance's two red parachutes could be
seen off the starboard wing to the north. Out the back through
the gaping hole the severed tail section came into view, tipped
on its side against the port elevator section, reminding all of
them, especially the captain of the aircraft, that the bodies of
two of his men were in that wreckage. Fortunately the tail
section had slewed sideways, so at this moment what was left
of their bodies could not be seen. That horrible mess would be
dealt with soon enough.

Beyond the tail section to the east, Robins saw the ridge
over which the VC-10 had dropped, breaking the tail section
off. That ridge looked as though it might be an esker. "Right,
chaps," he cried, "let's get on with finding an esker and
getting the airstrip staked out. That ridge back there," he
said, pointing, "looks like one. However, I'm sure there'll be

others around. But let's try that one first. Jason, you stay here and monitor the radio. Call me if there's anything urgent. Otherwise, take down the messages and I'll deal with it when I get back.

"Major LaFrance, would you be good enough to go and fetch the two parachutes. Bring them over to that ridge. Mr. Prentice, Cranston, and I will meet you there. Can you manage both of them?"

"No trouble at all."

"Good. Mr. Prentice, would you be good enough to come with Cranston and me. We may need some help clearing the landing area."

Arriving at the ridge, Robins found that it was indeed an esker, an endless river bed of gravel. But at the point closest to the aircraft, it curved. It did not provide a long enough stretch to accommodate the expected STOL Otters. However, within three minutes' walk south along the gravel ridge, about 250 yards from the aircraft, Robins found what he was looking for: a straight and level stretch, which he paced off at 850 feet. A little short, but with absolutely clear approaches at each end, probably more than enough. The strip was, he estimated, about thirty-five feet wide. There were many small boulders on it, but between the four of them they could get those moved away in short order.

LaFrance was soon on the scene with his two parachutes. After consultation on the location of the northern end of the strip to be cleared, the smaller chute was spread out and folded in the shape of the head of an arrow, with the head pointing south. Rocks were laid at each corner and along the edges.

Robins and LaFrance, with the second parachute tucked under his arm, walked to the southern portion of the selected landing area, while Prentice and Cranston started to work clearing the large stones. At the south end, the parachute was laid out, folded in the shape of a rectangle, and stretched lengthwise across the runway. By this time a five- to ten-mile-an-hour wind had come up from the southeast, a crosswind which the Otters could easily deal with, Robins guessed. By 3:30 they had cleared almost all the landing strip and the fog had totally dispersed. They were working in the light of a high, bright mid-summer sun, perspiring furiously as they heaved the heavy rocks off to the side of the esker.

Their work was finished to the satisfaction of the squadron leader just before four o'clock. As they made their way back to the wrecked machine, Robins stopped in his tracks, his right ear cocked to the east. His sensitive ears had detected the first sounds of approaching aircraft. In a few seconds more, the distant sound of large piston-driven engines and their throbbing propellers became distinct. "It's the Otters, all right."

Robins broke into a run toward the aircraft, getting himself to the VHF radio set as quickly as he could. He picked up the microphone. "CanForce Otters, this is VC-10 on Baker Lake frequency 201. How do you read?"

The response was immediate. "VC-10, this is Otter leader. We have you in sight about ten miles back. Have you a landing area for us?"

Now the Prime Minister stood anxiously at Robins' elbow in the cockpit. "Affirmative Otter leader. We've cleared a strip for you on an esker about 300 yards south of our aircraft. We've cleared about 900 feet. It's about thirty-five feet wide. We've marked each end with two red parachutes, which you should be able to see shortly."

The Otter leader came back, "Right, I've got them. It looks good. Each of us will do a low pass to take a look at the surface. I will land first. My instructions are to lift out all of you except Major LaFrance. I'll take you direct to Baker Lake. The Herc is already there waiting for you.

"I won't shut down the engine, so please approach the

THE OTTER
DEHAVILLAND AIRCRAFT OF CANADA LTD.

aircraft with great care and from the rear. The second aircraft will wait until we're airborne again before he lands. He's rigged with two litters to take the bodies of your crewmen. My instructions are the doctor will be responsible for supervising the job of getting them in a condition to move. I suggest if you haven't got anything to wrap them in you might use the parachutes. When the bodies and the personal effects are on board, the aircraft with the doctor will also proceed directly to Baker Lake. The Herc has brought in the RAF Board of Inquiry team so you and your crew should expect to remain in Baker Lake for the next few days."

To Robins, this last information was not unexpected. He could see a court martial and termination of a lifetime career facing him. He showed no emotion as he responded, "Roger, Otter leader. We'll move to the airstrip immediately."

The pounding roar of the two oncoming aircraft and the perpetual attraction of flying machines that lures every pilot compelled Squadron Leader Robins to join the other five men who were standing on the tundra, just outside the port door. Eyes squinting as they looked up into the brilliant blue, sun-filled Arctic sky, they watched the two ungainly, high-winged, silver-coloured Otters, enormous balloon tires hanging below. The planes bore down on them in close formation for a low pass. Thundering past the wreckage of the VC-10, the lead aircraft broke sharply to the left, turning south. The pilot circled to carry out a low, slow inspection of the marked esker surface.

It was the Prime Minister who moved back into the aircraft first, saying, "Right chaps, let's get organized and out to the strip." The group moved quickly to get their belongings together and out the door of the VC-10 for the final time, LaFrance carrying the Prime Minister's briefcase and suit-case. Robins asked LaFrance to turn off the radio and master switches when he was ready to board the second Otter; the

VC-10 captain would be back here with the members of the Board of Inquiry, and having power for radio contact with Baker Lake during that return visit would be essential.

As Robins left the aircraft, he saw the lead Otter, full flaps down, in STOL configuration rounding out its final landing approach. It touched down with a perfect three-point landing, not five feet beyond the arrowhead-shaped parachute. The sound of screaming brakes could be heard across the tundra as the Otter came to a halt a third of the way down the landing area. The aircraft did a 180° turn and then proceeded back to the north end of the strip. When it reached the arrowhead parachute another 180° turn brought it to a position facing down the strip, ready for the take-off. The rear door flew open to receive its passengers, who were climbing up the bank of the esker to the waiting machine.

A sergeant in a green Canadian Armed Forces flying suit jumped to the ground and leaned back against the door to hold it open against the propeller wash. "Just throw in your bags," he shouted at the group. "I'll tie them down when everybody's on board."

With that LaFrance threw the Prime Minister's gear up onto the cabin floor, then turned to help Sands step up into the machine. The Prime Minister had no problem, vigorously grabbing the handle on the right-hand side of the door and hoisting himself up and in. Inside the Otter, Sands turned back to LaFrance standing on the ground beneath him, held out his hand, and shouted above the noise of the engine and the propeller as they shook hands. "Thank you, Major. I shall not forget what you've done for me."

The last VC-10 survivor into the Otter was the captain. Like the others, he shook hands with LaFrance, thanking him for his aid. Then the Otter crewman leapt into the cabin. He slammed the passenger door shut and began tying the baggage down.

The Otter was rigged with four collapsible seats along the right side of the cabin, and two on the left side. The crewman's seat was on the left side at the rear, where he had access to a junction box into which he plugged the earphones and microphone attached to his crash helmet for communication with the pilot.

All the passengers had immediately gone to the first available seat and strapped themselves in. Sands required assistance because of his broken arm. Robins moved quickly up to him in his seat just behind the door to the cockpit. He strapped the Prime Minister in, then stuck his head into the cockpit to have a word with the two pilots, the captain on the left and the co-pilot on the right. Both wore formidable-looking white crash helmets and the green flying suit of the Canadian Armed Forces.

Squadron Leader Robins clapped the captain on the shoulder as he shouted, "Delighted to see you. You people are certainly a sight for sore eyes." The pilot smiled back at him and gave the traditional thumbs-up signal. As Robins withdrew his hand from the captain's shoulder, he saw the insignia of his rank: a crown above a crossed sword and baton; below that a single maple leaf – a brigadier general! These Canadians certainly did things differently, letting generals fly around the Arctic in single engine piston-driven aircraft!

He said nothing, but scuttled back to his seat on the right-hand side of the aircraft, sat down and put his safety belt on. By that time the crewman had finished tying down the baggage and had checked to ensure that all passengers were securely strapped in. He then reported ready to the captain, who immediately ran the engine up to take-off power. Then, with full take-off flap down, he released the brakes. The aircraft quickly began its take-off roll. The tail came up, and after an unbelievably short distance the Otter lifted off the esker. At fifty-five knots air speed the pilot brought the flaps

209

up to the climb position, easing back the power to a normal climb when sixty-five knots had been reached. Then he turned to starboard onto a compass heading of 330° for Baker Lake. They would be there in half an hour.

"Baker Lake, this is Otter leader. I'm out of the crash site at sixteen hundred hours, estimating Baker Lake at sixteen thirty-five. Have the Prime Minister on board."

"Roger Otter leader," called the same voice the crash survivors had depended on for so long. "Would you tell the Prime Minister there is an urgent call for him from the President of the United States. There is no telephone out at our airstrip but he could interconnect by telephone from the Herc by using its radio. On the other hand, if he wants some privacy and there are other calls he wants to make, he can come into our building in town."

"Okay Baker Lake. I'll ask him what he wants to do. Stand by one."

The general reached over his left shoulder to the radio jackbox switch which he turned to intercom. He looked at his co-pilot and pressed the transmit button on the butt end of his control wheel. "Ron, would you go back and pass the message to the Prime Minister and ask him what he wants to do? It's about two miles from the strip into town."

"Okay, sir." The co-pilot unlocked his harness, unplugged his crash helmet, squeezed out of the right-hand seat, and moved back into the cabin to kneel beside the Prime Minister and shout into his ear. In a few moments he was back in his seat in the cockpit. After strapping himself in and reconnecting his radio/intercom plug from his helmet, he pressed the transmit button. "He wants to go into the radio hut to use the telephone."

The pilot immediately switched to transmit.

"Baker Lake, Otter leader. The P.M. wants to come into your shop and use the telephone."

"Roger, Otter leader. The local administrator will be at the strip to drive him in. I'm sure the Herc has monitored this discussion. Rescue 316, have you heard what they've been saying?"

"Yes Baker Lake, we have."

Then the general switched back to intercom, pressed the button and said to his co-pilot, "Now you can see why the P.M. wants to use the telephone. If he talks to the President on the radio, the whole world can hear. If he uses the telephone and the satellite, only the Russians will be listening – maybe."

5:00 PM
The Cabinet Room, Centre Block
House of Commons
Ottawa, Canada

The Prime Minister had been prompt in getting his briefing underway. He was pleased to see that while it was not mandatory for any of the Cabinet ministers to appear, they were all there, every last one of them, some having travelled from other continents to get back in time.

As directed by Roussel, the briefing would be conducted by the senior civil servant in the Ottawa structure, the Secretary of the Cabinet and Clerk of the Privy Council, Norman Philips, a fluently bilingual protégé of the Prime Minister and a holder of a doctorate from the London School of Economics. Philips had initiated his career in the Department of External Affairs, then went to Industry, Trade, and Commerce as an assistant deputy minister, then deputy minister. The short, intense, round-faced, brown-haired man displayed much confidence in himself. He had often caught Roussel's eye and ear with his excellent ability to make concise presentations on the most difficult of subjects. When it had come time for the previous Clerk of the Privy Council to step down, the Prime Minister had reached through the maze of much more senior candidates, plucked Philips out of his deputy's chair, and lifted him to the heady heights of the Secretary's post.

For this presentation, the Prime Minister sat in his usual chair at the end of the long Cabinet table, while Philips was at the opposite end. The ministers were arranged on each side of the Cabinet table in order of seniority. In front of each was a pile of reports which had been assembled under Philips' direction. His job was to summarize what was in the material and to answer questions. Depending on the nature of the question put to him, he had available for assistance the deputy ministers of Labour, Urban Affairs, Defence, Transport, Finance, External Affairs, and Manpower and Immigration, and the president of the Central Mortgage and Housing Corporation.

The Prime Minister opened the proceedings by asking Norman Philips to make his presentation. Arching his thick, bushy eyebrows, Philips wasted no time.

"Prime Minister, ladies and gentlemen, in accordance with the instructions of the Prime Minister, the various departments have been studying and preparing answers to a list of questions relating to whether or not Canada could cope with a sudden influx of immigrants from Great Britain, and how that task might be accomplished. The terms of reference provide for two million people arriving within a period of one year. The top document on the pile in front of each of you is my summary of the material that is underneath."

The Prime Minister broke in. "I might say that I've read all the material. I consider your document to be an excellent summary in point form."

"Thank you, sir." Philips was pleased. "The first set of questions deals with where these people would go in Canada if directed, or if not directed; that is, the question of what accommodation facilities of any kind are available.

"In our opinion, they must be directed to, that is to say,

assigned to communities, and a mechanism must be established for the giving of such direction and the policing of its enforcement. Statistics show that if left to their own devices, probably three-quarters of them would wind up in Toronto, Hamilton, Winnipeg, Edmonton, Calgary, and Vancouver areas. This is unacceptable for any number of reasons. On the other hand, all of those areas will be required to take a very large number because that is where accommodation and employment are most readily available. We have ruled out Montreal because these are English-speaking people and we doubt that, under the present circumstances, many would go there.

"Our first recommendation, therefore, is that all immigrants from Great Britain under the open-gate policy, if adopted, should be assigned to specific communities and that the Ministry of State for Urban Affairs be responsible for devising an assignment plan and administering it.

"The next question has to do with accommodation. Most of the immigrants will be in family units, averaging between three and four people. Roughly speaking, this means we will have to find between 500,000 and 600,000 family accommodation units, and about 300,000 accommodation units for single persons. This, of course, would not be all at once. It will be phased over the year. This would give us a chance to mobilize and organize the space."

A question came from the Minister of Agriculture. "Where in heaven's name would you find all this accommodation? Our housing starts in Canada are expected to be below 138,000 this year. Do you really think we could find the space for two million people?"

There was no hesitation in Philips' response. "Yes, sir, I do. But it's not going to be the kind of accommodation you might have in your mind. Housing starts are one thing, but they'll be for the Canadian buyer. Most of the British people

214

who come here will have little or no money, and those who do bring some savings will have had their value cut in half by the collapse of the pound this week. You must remember, sir, these people are getting off the Islands because of dire need.

"Now, the kind of space we're looking at falls under several categories: First, we believe there are thousands of farmers across Canada who desperately need help and have houses large enough to take a family unit, especially if their accommodation is subsidized by government at least for a period of months. I'll come to the matter of financing later, Prime Minister."

Roussel nodded his acknowledgement.

"Secondly, in cities and urban areas there are hundreds of thousands of houses which have sufficient divided space to accommodate, temporarily, a second family; houses with recreation rooms, with toilet facilities attached; or a bedroom or two with bathroom facilities. In our calculation the key is the bathroom. We had fast telephone polls done yesterday and this morning right across the country, and only single-family home owners were approached. This includes the semi-detached, or the rural house, and townhouses as well. The question asked was: 'Do you have one or two rooms with a bathroom attached or available which could be used as a separate accommodation for an incoming British family for a minimum of twelve months, subject to a reasonable rental charge and a possible special income tax exemption?'

"The projections are that between 400,000 and 500,000 family accommodation units will be available across Canada. Now this is not just in the big cities, this also includes the very small towns and villages as well. And it also means that the incoming family people will have to go to the communities to which they are directed."

The Prime Minister asked, "What's this tax exemption you're talking about?"

"I would appreciate it, sir, if I could deal with that when I come to the question of cost and financing." The Prime Minister agreed, and Philips continued.

"A third type of accommodation is at military bases which are either still in operation or closed down across the country. For example, Camp Borden, just north of Toronto. This is the kind of place that could be used as a reception centre for the incoming people. They could be processed there and then sent out to their assigned communities. Similar temporary accommodation exists at Rockcliffe and, as I say, many other locations across the country. The Chief of the Defence Staff has indicated that the military will do their utmost to facilitate the opening of such accommodation, and the processing and handling of the incoming people."

The Minister of National Defence spoke up. "I think, Prime Minister, that the military would probably be the best in-place organization to call on if it is decided to let these people in." He decided to give Roussel a bit of a shaft. "The government has given the Canadian Armed Forces every other task and no money to do it with, so you might as well throw this one in on top."

The Prime Minister smiled and snorted, but said nothing in response. He motioned to Philips to continue.

"Other accommodation possibilities are mobile homes, trailers, and recreational vehicles. There are thousands of these units across the country which are used basically only in the summer season. We're trying to get a handle on the numbers from the various provincial governments' transportation ministries, where these vehicles are registered. And there are hundreds of trailer parks with sanitary sewage systems and water.

"The final major accommodation opportunity – there are many others, but we've tried to hit the main ones here – is the hotels, big and small. There are hundreds of small ones in

216

communities from coast to coast and most of them would be delighted to be assured of a full house for the next year or two at reasonable rates.

"So our report to you, Prime Minister, is that we believe there is sufficient accommodation available to house at least approximately two million immigrants from the United Kingdom. If you decide to accept the open-gate immigration policy, we would recommend that the receiving and processing of these people be the overall responsibility of Manpower and Immigration, in co-operation with the Department of National Defence. They would look after transportation to the community of assignment and the Ministry of State for Urban Affairs would be responsible for arranging accommodation, settling of rental charges, and other matters related to housing. Manpower and Immigration would, of course, be responsible for the paperwork and administration and would also be responsible through its employment arm for finding jobs for the workforce."

The Minister of Labour asked, "How many people out of this two million group would be employable?"

Philips replied, "Your people estimate between 700,000 and 800,000 of which 60 per cent would be unskilled."

"That many unskilled?"

"Yes, sir. The edition of *The Economist* issued on the 26th of October, 1974, included a chart – I have a copy here – showing that, of the unemployed workforce in the U.K. at that time, 60 per cent were unskilled. Those percentages are still valid today. It is largely this group which will be forced to emigrate, so we calculate that at least 60 per cent will be unskilled."

The Minister of Labour broke in. "Which indicates we should be getting them out into the west – the farming area. And into Alberta and British Columbia and the Northwest Territories, what with the Mackenzie Valley natural gas

217

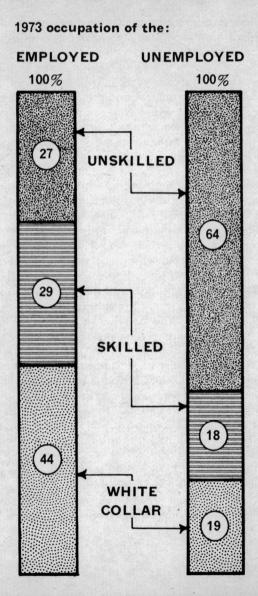

THE UNSKILLED DOLE

1973 occupation of the:

EMPLOYED   UNEMPLOYED
100%   100%

UNSKILLED

27   64

SKILLED

29

18

WHITE
COLLAR

44   19

pipeline coming on, and the crude oil pipeline from the Mackenzie delta a good prospect."

"That's perfectly correct, sir. And furthermore, as you well know, British Columbia and Alberta have taken – how shall I put it – have taken a very strong position in favour of the open-gate immigration policy."

It was the Minister of Labour's turn to snort. "You don't have to tell me. I'm from B.C. and I've had that fellow, Bullit, down my throat every hour on the hour."

The Minister of Agriculture spoke up again. "And what have the labour unions got to say about all these people coming in on top of them?"

"It's by no means unanimous, but by and large, the unions have said, 'Let them come, we'll sort it out when they get here.' Frankly, I found this attitude a little hard to believe until it was pointed out to me that in the last ten to twenty years, British immigrants have taken over most of the top positions in the Canadian unions."

"I'll say it if no one else will," the Prime Minister interjected. "That probably accounts for Canada having the worst strike record in the free world, except for Italy. I was looking at the figures the other day. Shocking. If I can remember the numbers in the period of 1969 to 1973, the average number of working days lost per thousand employees in mining, manufacturing, construction, and transport was Italy 2,200, Canada about 1,700, the U.S. less than 1,400, and Britain just over a thousand. Mind you the Canadian Labour Congress says those figures are all wrong."

"Surely, if we have such a large workforce," the Minister of Transport asked, "you say about 700,000, dumped on us all at once, it's going to take two or three years before the labour market can absorb these people, if it can in that period of time. And if that's the case, won't most of these people be on welfare and won't we have to support them?"

AVERAGE NUMBER OF WORKING DAYS LOST PER THOUSAND EMPLOYEES IN MINING, MANUFACTURING, CONSTRUCTION, AND TRANSPORT

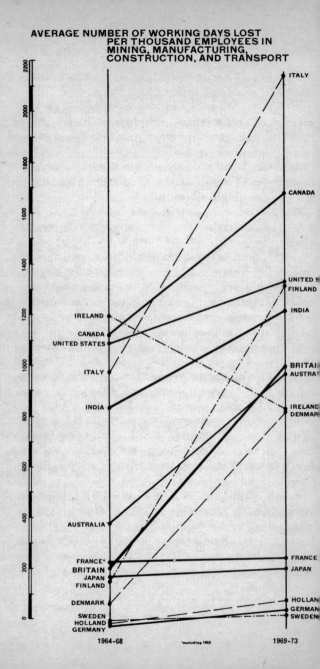

1964-68		1969-73
		ITALY
		CANADA
IRELAND		UNITED S
CANADA		FINLAND
UNITED STATES		INDIA
ITALY		BRITAI
INDIA		AUSTRA*
		IRELAND
		DENMAR
AUSTRALIA		FRANCE
FRANCE*		JAPAN
BRITAIN		
JAPAN		
FINLAND		
DENMARK		HOLLAN
SWEDEN		GERMAN
HOLLAND		SWEDEN
GERMANY		

*excluding 1968

The Deputy Minister of Labour, sitting with the other deputies against the wall on Norman Philips' right, scuttled over to Philips and spoke to him in a whispered voice. Then Philips replied to the Minister. "We don't think it will be as long as you suggest before they're absorbed into the market. If our figure of at least 60 per cent unskilled is true, and if we don't support them by welfare to such an extent that it's more profitable for them not to work . . ."

"So what else is new," someone down the Cabinet table remarked.

" . . . and if these people are in fact prepared to work, we believe that there are hundreds of thousands of unskilled job opportunities across the country. We've seen western Europeans come into this country by the hundreds of thousands, prepared to work with their hands. They've had no trouble at all making their way, because they're prepared to work."

By this time the Prime Minister noticed that while all of the Cabinet ministers from Quebec were present, not one of them had asked a question. The only negative questions came from Ontario M.P.s, particularily those from the Golden Horseshoe area from Toronto to Hamilton. He made no remark about his observation, but said instead, "Mr. Philips, can we now talk about the cost of all this?"

Before Philips could answer, the Minister of Urban Affairs, a strong individual from the key Great Lakes port of Thunder Bay, intervened. "I want to make a suggestion here, Prime Minister. We've been talking about putting these people into existing urban communities. That's fine, but I think we should also be looking at building some new towns, using this new workforce to do it. We've heard a lot about a plan called the Mid-Canada Development Corridor, which is a scheme for the future planning and development of the entire boreal forest. That's the northern forest which stretches from coast to coast in Canada, between Canada South and the untreed bare

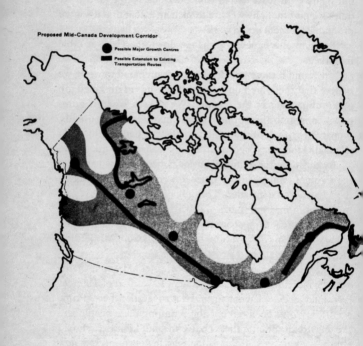

Proposed Mid-Canada Development Corridor

● Possible Major Growth Centres

▬ Possible Extension to Existing
Transportation Routes

Arctic area. We've never moved on developing plans for the Mid-Canada region, but a lot of work has already been done. If the government decides to take all these people, I think we should do a crash program on the Mid-Canada concept."

The Prime Minister agreed. "Excellent idea. That plan was put forward by some lawyer from Toronto wasn't it? I've forgotten his name. Now, Mr. Philips, the finance question."

"The tax incentive we propose in order to make it attractive for people to rent out accommodation is simply that any rents they receive will be deductible and not taxed as income. The government of the U.K. has agreed to pay the cost of transportation across. We have a tentative agreement that they will also pay to the government of Canada a two-year subsidy of $500 per person per year, provided that: the money is used for the direct support of that person until the family becomes self-sufficient; and the maximum paid to any family unit shall not exceed $3,000 in any one year; and the Canadian government will at least match the U.K. subsidy. There would be, of course, a sliding scale for single persons, although we want to be careful not to encourage people to live together on an unmarried basis."

There were some further snorts around the Cabinet table.

"In any event, it looks to us as though the average cost of subsidy will be $700 per year, or 1.4 billion dollars. On the other hand, between now and the end of this current fiscal year next March 31st, not all of the immigrants would have arrived; they would come gradually, rather than en masse. So our potential expenditure during that period would be about 570 million dollars. During the following fiscal year, with all of the immigrants arrived in Canada – we're still talking two million – you will have a good portion of them already absorbed into the labour market, and therefore self-sufficient. So we ballpark the cost during the fiscal year commencing

April 1st at about a billion dollars; after that, the cost should drop rapidly as these people begin to work.

"If the government decides in favour of the open-gate immigration policy, Prime Minister, it is our recommendation that the entire budget of the Canadian International Development Agency, which is now approaching a billion dollars, be diverted to this use. In a comparable context we also recommend that immigration from all other countries other than the U.K. be cut off forthwith for a period of at least two years, except for people having special professional skills or trades, and then only under exceptional circumstances."

"I can certainly see a big fight over that one," the Prime Minister commented.

Roussel began gathering together the papers on the table in front of him, obviously preparing to leave. "While you've been making your presentation, Mr. Philips, you may have observed that I've had several messages handed to me, some of which are most urgent. It should not come as a surprise that the Premier of Quebec wishes to speak with me, the National Assembly having unanimously passed their secession resolution of which you are all aware. I guess he wants to hammer home his point a little further. There are also calls from the Premiers of Ontario, British Columbia, and Alberta, so I have my work cut out for me. I would be obliged, Mr. Philips, if you and your associates would carry on and make yourselves available for further questions from my colleagues. I know you haven't quite finished your presentation, but you've covered the main points which concern me. Ladies and gentlemen, I will see you at the Cabinet meeting in this room at eight."

As he stood up to leave, he said in a sarcastic tone, "Now I'll go and talk with the Premier of Ontario to find out if they too have decided to secede."

Dead ahead, the west end of Baker Lake could be seen across the brown tundra rolling by beneath the slow-moving Otter.

"Baker Lake, Otter leader. I'm five to the southeast at 2,000. Landing."

"Right, Otter leader. I have no local traffic. The wind is from the southeast, five to ten miles an hour. Altimeter setting three zero decimal one three."

"Roger. I'll land from south to north, downwind." The downwind landing would put the Otter opposite the taxiway nearest the parking area at the north end of the strip.

The general made another smooth-as-silk landing, provoking friendly but needling jibes from both the co-pilot and crewman. He responded jokingly, threatening instant demotion for both of them. As soon as the Otter was shut down in the parking area next to the prefabricated metal building at its eastern end, the Prime Minister and Prentice were out of the aircraft. Prentice muttered to the Prime Minister about getting to the hospital, but Sands waved him off. They climbed into the local administrator's vehicle and started for the distant village of Baker Lake, over the bumpy, dusty, rutted gravel road which skirts the west end of the lake. As they drove eastward through the village, the administrator pointed out the sights: the RCMP building on the south, the Hudson's Bay store, the hospital, and the Eskimo housing on the north. To Sands, the houses seemed almost exactly the same as those he had seen at Frobisher. Squalor was the word he would use to describe it. At the east end of the village they arrived at the radio shack, double-doored to keep out the mosquitoes in summer and the cold in winter. Sands and Prentice followed their host past guest bedrooms on each side of the entrance and into the radio room itself, which looked out onto the lake.

The Prime Minister thanked the radio operator on duty, as well as his two partners who had turned up for this special occasion, for the assistance they had given him over the hours since the crash. But the important thing was to get the President on the line. Sands spoke to him from the privacy of a newly installed telephone in one of the sleeping rooms down the hall. It was shortly before five local time; Washington was an hour later.

After expressions of concern about the Prime Minister's health, the President got right to the point. He was never one to fail to express what was on his mind. "Your people and mine are making progress Jeremy, but I want to tell you that this fellow, Hobson, doesn't do you much credit. We've had one hell of a time with him. Frankly, he's not very bright. I don't think he understands the ramifications of some of the things he says you want us to do. And as a matter of fact, on some of the issues, I've had to argue for your position against my own people."

Sands said nothing in response, but merely shook his head silently in disgust.

The President continued. "Anyway, we've got the short term monetary problems resolved. Both the International Monetary Fund and OECD fund monies and credits will be

226

available to you immediately on our guarantee. I won't go into the details now. Jessica will do that when she meets you in Ottawa."

The Prime Minister was surprised. "She's meeting me in Ottawa?"

"Yes, she'll be there when you arrive. I want her to talk to you before you see Roussel, so when you meet with him you'll have been fully briefed on the position of the United States government, what we're prepared to do. But of course you'll want to get to the hospital before you see her."

"No way I'm going to any bloody hospital," Sands interjected.

"It may be just as well. There'll probably be some additional points to clear up that only you can handle. She'll tell you about her visit to Saudi Arabia. She saw the King yesterday. He might relent."

"I doubt it," Sands responded pessimistically.

Sheppard disregarded Sands' remark. "Now the reason I wanted to talk with you Jeremy, is simply this. The United States' support of the U.K., the monetary support, everything, has a hooker to it. I can't get this guy Hobson to buy it, even though it's fundamental to the long-term survival of Great Britain – at least I think it is. What we've said to him is this: you people have billions of barrels of proved reserves of crude oil in the North Sea. Once you get those fields into production, you'll have enough crude oil to meet all your own needs and you'll likely have a surplus for export. When that day arrives, you can thumb your nose at the Arabs. Your balance of payments deficits will be out of the way. So, it's absolutely essential that those North Sea fields be developed and pipelines built to bring that stuff onshore as quickly as possible. But your country just can't do it. You've had continuing strikes in the pipeline-building trades, the firms that build the floating drilling rigs, and the unions that do the drilling itself. The British companies which have been responsible for management of the development have collapsed. As I said to you when we talked earlier this week, instead of getting the oil onshore by the original target date, the way you're going you'll never get it there."

Sands interrupted. "Yes, and as I recall our conversation, I said it was too late and there was nothing we could do about it."

"Yes, that's right, but there is something you can do about it and this is what it is. By the way, Hobson refuses to go along with the proposition I am going to put to you but it's fundamental to the whole deal."

The Prime Minister glanced at his suitcoat pocket for the pipe he normally kept there. The pocket was empty. He had left the pipe on the VC-10 in the rush to leave.

"The position we're taking is this: you people have to get yourselves back on your feet. The only way to do it is to get your crude oil onshore fast. We can't afford to carry you if you don't. You obviously haven't got the capability to put it all together. What we're saying is that you must agree to allow the government of the United States to take over the task of building the pipelines, developing the fields, and putting in place the entire mechanism for delivering North Sea crude oil onshore in the United Kingdom. That means American engineers, American equipment, American pipes, American know-how. You'll pay us for it out of revenue over the next ten or twenty years. We'll hire the people here in the States. The work force will be totally American. I don't want the British trade unions involved in any way, shape, or form. We'll have the oil flowing in eighteen months."

Sands said nothing. His mind was sorting out the implications of what the President was saying.

"I've made a deal with Venezuela and with the Shah that they'll up their production in order to supply you with your crude oil needs during that period; so an interim supply is no problem. And the United States will finance the purchase of those supplies. But Jeremy, and I'm repeating myself, the hooker is that you've got to get your own North Sea crude oil onshore. You can't do it yourselves and in the interests of both the United States and the United Kingdom, you'll have to let us do it."

The line was silent for a moment. A mosquito buzzed by Sands' ear as he sat in the dingy Baker Lake room, weighing a proposal which would have enormous effects upon his country and its future. After a moment he said, "Mr. President, that's an offer I cannot refuse."

The Prime Minister then asked to speak with the Chancellor of the Exchequer. After Hobson's inquiries after Sands' well-being, the Prime Minister took him to task for not consulting the Cabinet during the course of his negotiations in Washington. The Chancellor responded that he felt it would be much better for him to make an agreement subject to Cabinet confirmation, then take it back to them in London. Besides, the problem was so complex and he was right on top of the situation. In any event, the Prime Minister had really been out of touch since the crash so Hobson had to press on by himself.

Sands would not go for this argument. "You know very well you could have got through to me by radio!"

"Yes, Prime Minister, but . . ."

Sands broke in on him. "You mean, 'Yes, but I chose to do it my own way.' Frankly, I find your conduct and attitude unacceptable. I don't want to deal with this subject any further until I see you." The Prime Minister had to get on with settling arrangements with the Americans. That was the important thing.

"The President informs me," Sands continued, "that you

don't like their proposal regarding development of the North Sea oil fields."

"That's right," Hobson responded, "the unions would never stand for it."

This was the answer the Prime Minister had expected. "Although the unions would like to govern the country and may be very close to achieving that objective, they haven't done so yet. It's the unions who have brought our North Sea potential virtually to nought, with their internal fighting, bickering, and strikes over which union should be doing what. The Americans have already had to take over the development of the Ninian field from Burmah when it collapsed in 1974.

"No, Michael, the unions are interested only in themselves, and for the most part, so far as I can see, the trade union leaders are interested only in feathering their own nests. They don't give a damn for the poor devils in their membership or for the country. The government must act in the interests of all of the people, whether they're trade union bosses or members of trade unions or not. Getting the North Sea oil onshore as quickly as possible is a matter of life and death for Great Britain. Getting a continuing supply until that time – until we become self-sufficient – is also a matter of life and death for us. This is simply not a situation we can muddle through. I've told the President that under the circumstances, I have no choice but to accept the American proposal. Now while that may be contrary to the position you've taken, Mr. Chancellor, I expect you to support me. I've given you the reasons why I think we must go along with the United States. They cut right across your line of thinking. However, if you cannot accept my position, I will expect you to resign from the Cabinet, in fact I am prepared to accept your resignation by telephone at this very moment!"

Sands knew what Hobson's answer would be. The Chancellor was a lover of power and pomp. He would have no difficulty in justifying a reversal of his North Sea position if it meant that sticking with a principle would result in his departure from the Cabinet.

"Heavens, Prime Minister," he demurred. "No need to talk of resignation. I understand your reasoning about the unions perfectly and I am prepared to support you completely."

"That's jolly good, Michael. Now I want you to be nothing but sweetness and light with the Americans. Get the proposal wrapped up as quickly as possible. I understand from the President that almost all the details have been sorted out with the exception of this one point. The Secretary of State wants to meet me when I get to Ottawa. So, time is short. I understand the President wants her to cover with me the terms of the deal you're working on. He and I didn't discuss the United States' decision on the open-gate immigration request. Have you had any indication as to what their thinking is on this as yet?"

"Not a clue. I haven't any idea what they're going to do. They've asked me a few questions about numbers of people, that kind of thing. My understanding is that the President is negotiating with the appropriate congressional leaders. His staff are trying to get readings from people all across the country as to how they would react if they had a flood of Brits coming in."

The radio operator knocked on the door, entered without waiting, handed the Prime Minister a slip of paper, and left. "Your wife is on the line," it read.

"Michael, I must go. Will you come to Ottawa with the Secretary?"

"I don't mind, Prime Minister, but I'd like to get back to London as soon as I'm finished here. I've been away too long already. They've been going mad dealing with crisis questions by telephone, day and bloody night."

231

The Prime Minister understood. "Quite so, Michael. Yes, yes. Very well then. I'll see you in London."

Sands then had a brief but reassuring and warm conversation with his dear wife, Mary, who in her own way had shared her husband's suffering across the thousands of miles between them. But never mind. He was safe. His only injury was a broken arm and he would soon be on his way home.

As he put down the telephone, the Prime Minister slumped forward slightly. He was tired. His left arm was giving him a great deal of pain. Time to get a move on. Pulling himself together, he stood up, a little unsteady on his feet for a moment. Then he left the shabby little room and went back to the radio office, where Prentice and the administrator were waiting for him.

"You all right, sir?" his secretary asked, concerned by Sands' haggard, grey-faced appearance.

Sands waved him off, smiling. "Actually, I'm in great shape, Prentice, thank you very much."

Turning to the radio operator, Sands said, "I want to thank you again for all you've done for me." He reached across the counter to shake hands with the young man, who beamed with pleasure.

"Thank you, sir. It was a privilege to meet you and to have a bit of a hand in the things that've been going on." He turned quickly toward the telex machine clattering behind him, saying, "There's a message from Prime Minister Roussel coming in on the telex now."

The machine stopped its chatter. The operator carefully ripped the green paper from the top of the unit and handed it to Sands, who, impaired though he was with the use of his right hand only, had already slipped on his glasses. He began to read.

The first part of the message expressed Roussel's pleasure that Sands had survived the crash and that the rescue operation had worked so successfully. He understood Sands was proceeding directly to Ottawa. Roussel would be pleased to see him as soon as he arrived. Yves Parent, the Minister for External Affairs, would meet him at Uplands Airport, Ottawa, on his arrival that evening. The telex went on:

> Regret unable to meet you at Uplands personally, but Cabinet will be in special emergency session to make decision on your request for open-gate immigration. Parent will take you to Ottawa General Hospital then on to my offices in the Parliament Buildings. Overnight accommodation arranged for you at the Chateau Laurier Hotel. Alternatively, Canadian Armed Forces 707 standing by to lift you to Washington or London. Regards. Roussel.

The Prime Minister whipped off his glasses and instructed Prentice, "I want to send a message back to him. Would you take it down please?"

Prentice quickly produced a pen and wrote the Prime Minister's message on the telex form on the counter.

> Thank you for your message of concern and for opportunity to see you. Urgently request privilege of meeting with Cabinet before final decision taken on immigration question so can answer questions, explain crisis and urgent need to move people out of U.K. Will not go to hospital at this time. Also, I commend Canadian Armed Forces, especially Air Reserve and Major LaFrance of the Canadian Airborne Regiment for outstanding work in rescue operation. Sands.

As Prentice handed the message to the operator, he turned to the Prime Minister and said, "Sir, the Captain of the Herc says it will take about four hours to get to Ottawa. It will take us fifteen minutes to drive back to the airstrip. So, if we get airborne at 5:30, that would put us into Ottawa about 10:30."

"We'd better get a move on!"

They left the radio shack immediately. Clattering and bumping along the rutted road through the village and around the end of the lake, they drove up to the airstrip where the squat Hercules sat. Its port passenger door was open to receive them, and its captain and loadmasters were standing beside the aircraft, talking with Squadron Leader Robins and his crew. As the Prime Minister's car approached, the Herc captain disappeared into the aircraft to prepare to start.

Farewells were quickly said. The stooped Prime Minister spoke with Basil Robins last. "What's happened to the Board of Inquiry investigating team that came in on the Herc? I wanted to have a word with them before they left but they seem to have disappeared."

"They're dead keen to get out to our aircraft, so the Otters are taking them out. They left about five minutes ago."

The Prime Minister looked up intently into the taller man's eyes. "Basil, the next few weeks will be very difficult for you." His voice rose to a near shout as the first of the starboard engines started up. "You did a masterful job in getting us down and handling the situation on the ground. I will so advise the Defence Secretary and your military superiors. Good luck." The two men shook hands.

The second starboard engine started up. The Prime Minister stepped up through the door of the Herc, assisted by the senior loadmaster, who said as Sands entered the cavernous fuselage, "Would you go up the stairs to the flight deck just to the left here, sir."

Sands, about to climb the steps up into the cockpit area, stopped short and turned to the crew chief. He pointed across to the two long bundles laid out on the canvas seats against the starboard wall of the cabin, asking, "What are those?"

"They're the two crewmen from the VC-10, sir." Without a word the Prime Minister moved up the steps.

234

8:00 PM
The Cabinet Room, Centre Block
Parliament Buildings
Ottawa, Canada

The Prime Minister of Canada looked around the Cabinet table. Satisfied, he said, "Ladies and gentlemen, I see we're all here. I anticipate that the exercise of deciding whether we should adopt an open-gate immigration policy will probably be the most divisive, difficult question this Cabinet has ever faced. With the positions taken by the governments of Quebec on the one hand and British Columbia and Alberta on the other, there appears to be no way we can win or that Confederation can be held together. On the other hand, I'm optimistic that whichever way this vote goes, we can persuade the dissenting provinces not to leave. That is a chance we have no choice but to take at this time.

"I propose that this meeting be conducted on a vote basis, and that the results of the vote be made public. This is contrary to the usual practice of the Cabinet. But it follows the precedent established when the Cabinet of the United Kingdom decided in March of 1975 during the referendum on the question that it would support the proposition of remaining in the European Economic Community. For myself, I propose to act as a neutral chairman. I will not take part in the debate and I will cast my vote only in the event of a tie.

"Now ladies and gentlemen, to begin the proceedings, I'm sure that one of you will be prepared to introduce a motion, either for or against adopting the open-gate immigration policy."

10:33 PM
Canadian Armed Forces Base Uplands
Ottawa International Airport
Canada

Prime Minister Sands had slept until the Hercules transport was about half an hour out of Ottawa. When he was assisted down from the bunk and strapped into a seat behind the co-pilot, he glanced on the floor beside him and spotted the *Ottawa Journal*. It was the headline that gave him his first shock: "QUEBEC TO SECEDE." The lead story began:

> The Quebec National Assembly is expected to vote today in support of a government resolution that Quebec secede from Confederation in the event the federal government decides in favour of the open-gate immigration policy requested by the government of the United Kingdom. The policy would allow a mass influx of some two million Britons into English-speaking Canada within the next twelve months.
>
> The resolution to secede will be considered in an emergency session of the Quebec National Assembly and will probably be presented by the Premier, Gaston Belisle.
>
> It is expected that the Premier of Quebec will meet with Prime Minister Roussel in Ottawa late Wednesday afternoon to communicate personally the decision of the

National Assembly. It is reported that he will emphasize the expected solidarity of all Quebec political parties in support of the resolution, and he will stress that there is no ground for negotiation.

In an interview, the Premier was asked for his reaction to the news that the British Columbia and Alberta Cabinets had decided that they would secede if the federal government refused to adopt the open-gate immigration policy. The Premier commented "It means Confederation is at an end, whichever way the federal government goes. On the other hand, I am confident that Mr. Roussel's government will make the right decision so far as Quebec is concerned."

Sands had been to British Columbia many times. It was the most British of all the provinces by far. He knew there had been talk of secession by British Columbia over the years: B.C. and Alberta had fought against the centralization of power in remote eastern Canada. But it was hard to believe that it had come to this.

He put down the newspaper and sat back in his chair, engulfed in the constant, steady throbbing of the turbo-prop engines. He did not hear them. How incongruous that Great Britain, the mother country responsible for putting Canada together, was now to be the cause for the break-up of Canada. Would it really come to that? Would there be no way to keep Canada together? Could his own government back off on the request for an open-gate immigration policy? For all the humane, social, and economic reasons he could think of, there was no way he could retreat. It was a people question. People. Hundreds of thousands of them, millions of them, having to survive, having to live, having to have food and work. No, the Canadians would just have to fight it out. With their vast land and enormous natural resources and their small population,

238

they could take the British immigrants. And they had ancient, close ties with Britain. Even the French-Canadians in Quebec had long-standing obligations to Great Britain, for England had been most lenient with the conquered French after the conclusive battle of the Plains of Abraham. No, he would not back off.

The Herc touched down in darkness at Ottawa International Airport at 10:33 PM. It turned off the runway, rolling north along the taxiway past the brightly illuminated terminal building, heading for the military Air Movements Unit terminal.

Looking over the co-pilot's shoulder, past the softly lit instrument panel, through the darkness Sands could see, silhouetted against the lights from the AMU building, two aircraft he recognized as Boeing 707s. Both of them were facing the building. One of them was an unpainted aircraft, its shining aluminum skin reflecting the lights of the building. That would be Air Force One, the President's aircraft which had brought in the Secretary of State. Its cabin lights were on, and its navigation lights as well. The other 707, Sands could now see, had Canadian Forces markings. It was sitting without any lights or any sign of activity. That was probably the aircraft which would take him back to the U.K. when his business in Ottawa was finished, or to Washington should he decide to go there.

As the Herc swung in toward the parking ramp from the taxiway, the pilot was marshalled in to swing round and stop next to Air Force One. Milling about on the grassed area in front of the Air Movements Unit building was a small crowd of people, held back by Royal Canadian Mounted Police officers.

The press, thought Prime Minister Sands, and why not? Then he noticed another little band of people being shepherded through the crowd, past the RCMP officers, moving

239

quickly around the port wing of the Herc. Sands by this time was unstrapped, standing, ready to make his way down the steps from the flight deck to the main cabin and out the port side. Rumpled and unsteady as he was, he managed a few words of thanks to the crew, then made his way down the steps from the flight deck to the exit door of the aircraft. He was greeted by the Canadian Minister for External Affairs, Yves Parent, whom Sands had not met before. Parent, a tall, balding man in his early fifties, with a prominent French-Canadian accent, was clearly anxious to have his part of the welcome over with so he could get away. After expressing his regret about the accident and the Prime Minister's injury, and after communicating the greetings and best wishes of the Prime Minister, Parent explained that the Cabinet was still in session. The way things were going when he had left a half hour before, it would be continuing for some time. In any event, it was imperative for him to get back to that meeting as quickly as possible, because of the importance of the decisions to be made, especially for Quebec.

Strange, thought the Prime Minister. I should have thought his concern would have been for Canada, not just Quebec.

Parent informed the Prime Minister that the Secretary of State was waiting for him in her aircraft, so as soon as Sands was finished with the press, Parent would escort him to Air Force One. The Prime Minister acknowledged the greetings, saying he was obliged to the Minister for his courtesy and kindness. The press conference would not last long. As soon as the Minister for External Affairs had delivered him to Air Force One, he would be obliged if Parent might feel free to return to the Cabinet meeting.

However, Sands knew intuitively that, in the interests of all the hundreds of thousands of Britons who would want to come to Canada to make their lives here, it would be best if

Parent was delayed as long as possible, perhaps even prevented from getting back to that crucial Cabinet meeting.

The press conference on the ramp in front of the Herc was noisy and kaleidoscopic as the lights of the television cameras followed the Prime Minister's slow procession toward Air Force One. Microphones were shoved in front of his face as questions were shot at him about the crash, the crisis, the position of the United States, and above all, his views on the deep division that had developed in Canada.

He responded by saying that the open-gate policy request was really no more than a reflection of the wishes of literally millions of Britons to get off the Islands, to go elsewhere in the world to make a new start. No better place existed than Canada, with its vast expanses of usable but unpopulated land, and with its resources, industry, food, and a lifestyle and system of government envied throughout the free world. All the United Kingdom could do is recognize not only that these people want to get off the Islands, but also that it was an important step toward a new beginning for the U.K.

What were his plans? Where was he going next? What would he say to the Prime Minister of Canada? Did he want to talk to the Cabinet about the open-gate policy? Did he want money from Canada? Did he think the Canadian economy could withstand the impact of two million new people in one year? What was the crash like? How about the broken arm? The questions were peppered at him from all sides. Sorting them out, he answered each of them briefly, all the while moving deliberately toward the American aircraft.

Finally Prime Minister Sands' little party reached the base of the steps leading up to the front port door of Air Force One. Sands' left arm had been jostled three times on the way across, so it was giving him a little more pain than usual. He would have to get it into a cast. It had taken him ten minutes to walk 120 feet, answering questions every inch of the way.

He mounted the steps. On the second one, bathed in brilliant camera lights, he turned to face the crowd, speaking so everyone could hear.

"I'm sorry I can't spend more time with you, but I must meet with the Secretary of State, who has been courteous enough to come here to see me to communicate the position of her government. I must see the Secretary and then get into Ottawa as quickly as possible. It is my express wish to attend before the Canadian Cabinet to explain our situation fully and to ask for the open-gate policy. I realize the great split that our request has made in the Cabinet and perhaps throughout Canada. However, these are times when uncertainty confronts all nations. None of us in the Western world, with our economies and our people tied so closely together, can function or operate independently of one another. All of us have moral and economic responsibilities which must be recognized. None can turn its back on the other. This great prosperous Canadian nation was built by a host of people of varying nationalities, races, colours, and creeds. It is a veritable patchwork of cultures. But the important point is that it has been built by immigrants and the sons and daughters of immigrants and the grandchildren of immigrants."

There was a perceptible hush as this eloquent Englishman spoke. Even though he was the leader of a shattered country, he was a man of commanding presence.

His voice rose as he concluded. "Canada is a magnificent country. I hope its people and its government are as rich in their souls as they are in their vast lands and resources and in the superb cities they have built. In the name of humanity, I hope your government will accept my plea on behalf of millions of Britons to let them come and be citizens and workers, contributors to the special way of life you have here, which is the envy of the free world."

With that, he leaned down to shake hands with Yves Parent, thanking him for his hospitality and saying expectantly that he would see him shortly. Parent said nothing. He merely looked at the Prime Minister coldly, his reponse to Sands' short speech etched on his stony face. Then the Minister turned and quickly disappeared into the crowd. Sands climbed slowly up the steps of Air Force One, followed by his faithful Prentice. The parting with Parent might have been cold, but Sands knew that the greeting at the top of those steps would be warm.

When he reached the entrance to the aircraft, he turned and waved to the people below, cameras and lights still trained on him. Just as he was about to cease waving and move into the cabin, he felt a light touch on his right arm. Half turning in the doorway, he looked directly into the face of Jessica Swift, the attractive Secretary of State of the United States of America. She was a woman he admired, respected and, indeed, loved, although that love was rarely ever expressed in any other way except perhaps a touch or a look. She had been so understanding, so helpful through the short months since she had become Secretary. As a result of their many meetings, in Washington, London, the Middle East, or the Soviet Union, he had become enormously fond of this superlative woman.

As for Jessica Swift, her feelings for this tough father-figure, this kind man, the leader of an harassed, faltering, stumbling, proud nation, was one of closeness and understanding. She responded directly to the feeling of affection which she could read on his face. She loved this man in the same way he loved her. And so when she stood back from the door as he waved to the crowd, not seeing her yet, the sight of his broken arm moved her to sympathy and compassion. On impulse, she had stepped forward to touch his arm. She embraced him as he turned toward her, her arms inside his so

243

as not to touch the injured limb. He planted a kiss on both her cheeks, all in full view of the cameras, recording for the world this uncontrived moment. Then without looking back to the crowd the two of them disappeared into the cabin of Air Force One, where Jessica led Sands to the private office area of the aircraft. She offered him a gentleman's-sized snifter of cognac, which he accepted. She also had a novel treat for him – she offered Sands a first-class Havana cigar, symbolic of the new trade relationship which she had been instrumental in developing with Cuba.

Sands settled back in the comfortable seat. He took a delicious puff of the cigar, and then a sip of the excellent cognac – Jessica thought it would be good for him. Jeremy Sands, his silver hair now groomed, his bushy white eyebrows lowered comfortably over his contented blue eyes, gazed across the small table at this magnificent person. "Jessica . . . you know, my dear, as of this moment I have returned to the land of the living. In fact, I feel almost Churchillian . . . cigar, brandy, and one of the most attractive women I've ever met."

She smiled at him with pleasure. "Ah, Jeremy, you do marvellous things for me, but you do such terrible things to my work load." They laughed together as she sipped her cognac. One thing about Jessica which always impressed Sands was that she could stay with any man when it came to alcohol, and had the happy, inexplicable ability to show little evidence of her drinking, even when she was with the Russians. She had told him about her bread and vodka trick.

"Now Jeremy, let's talk about that work load. I know you've got to get to the Cabinet meeting to make your pitch, so let me give it to you in a nutshell. The President and I were both of one mind that I should tell you face to face what we're prepared to do. By the way, the President was not at all happy about Michael Hobson. We think he's an opinionated,

244

stubborn man, really in well over his head. I suppose he did his best with limited ability. I'm sure he'll report to you fully when you get back to London. He's already on his way, as you know."

Sands nodded. "He may report to me, but frankly, I intend to replace him immediately."

The Secretary of State did not react. Instead, she stood up, crossed to the desk, picked up a document and returned. Sitting down again, she picked up her brandy, sipped, reached down to the floor, took out her glasses, put them on the end of her nose, and began to speak. "This is the memorandum of the agreement we reached with Hobson, subject to the approval of you and your government." She handed it to him. "Perhaps it would be easier if you read it. Then we can talk about it." She added, "I haven't heard anything from the King of Saudi Arabia, so I assume he's not going to relent. You can't win them all."

Sands understood. "Thank you for trying, Jessica." He put down his brandy to take the sheet from her and slipping on his glasses, began to read the document slowly and carefully.

MEMORANDUM OF AGREEMENT

The government of the United States (the U.S.) is desirous of assisting the people and government of the United Kingdom (the U.K.) during the current period of economic crisis. Subject to certain terms and conditions which are recited in this document, the U.S. government is prepared to give assistance in the form of financial support as well as both direct and indirect aid in obtaining a continuing supply of essential food, energy, and raw materials. It is the intent of both parties that the U.K. should achieve at the earliest possible moment both a new economic base and an energy self-sufficiency through the development of the North Sea crude oil fields. To these ends, and subject to the approval of the government of the U.K., which shall be communicated to the U.S. not later than twelve noon Washington time, on Thursday, July 8, the U.S. and the U.K. agree as follows:

1. The U.S. will forthwith lend to the U.K. twenty (20) billion dollars (U.S.) with interest at the prime New York bank rate, said loan to be repayable in ten equal annual instalments commencing on the first day of the third year after the first crude oil flows onshore by pipeline to the U.K. from the North Sea oilfields. Interest is to be waived until the said first day of the third year, thereafter to be payable annually.

2. The U.S. will support by guarantee the application of the U.K. to the International Monetary Fund for a loan of ten billion dollars (U.S.) which has already been arranged by the U.S., and to the OECD fund for a line of credit for an additional ten billion dollars (U.S.) which will be taken down as required by the U.K.

3. The U.S. will assist the U.K. in negotiating with Iran, Venezuela, and other non-Arab members of OPEC for a continued supply of crude oil, and will provide guarantees of payment should the same be requested by the governments of the producing countries, provided that a system of stringent rationing of gasoline by coupon shall be instituted forthwith by the U.K. and maintained until such time as crude oil self-sufficiency from North Sea production has been achieved.

The Prime Minister paused for a moment, looked over his glasses at Jessica Swift, and remarked with a smile, "The oil clause makes me happy. With the guarantee of your government on the table, it won't be necessary for me to go to

Teheran. My place right now is at 10 Downing Street. The sooner the better." He read further.

4. In consultation with the government of the U.K., the U.S. will make available from its own stocks, or will assist the U.K. in acquiring in world markets, essential foodstuffs necessary for the feeding of the people of the U.K., provided that the U.K. commits itself to a policy of curtailing, and wherever possible, stopping, the importation of luxury food and merchandise; and that the rationing of food by coupon be forthwith instituted and maintained at least until the aforesaid first day of the third year after the first flow of crude oil from the North Sea by pipeline.

Without looking up, Sands muttered, "We've already implemented the rationing of both petrol and food."

5. To the extent that any provisions of this memorandum are contrary to the agreements which the U.K. has with its partners in the European Economic Community and the EEC does not grant its consent to the U.K. to enter into this agreement or any part thereof, then the U.K. will forthwith withdraw from the EEC and take all legislative and other steps necessary to effect such withdrawal.

6. In order to expedite the delivery of product from the North Sea crude oil fields, the U.K. agrees to retain a consortium of U.S. engineering, pipelining, well-drilling, marine, and other specialists for the purpose of developing the North Sea crude oil fields and designing, building, and operating the pipelines and other transportation systems necessary to find, extract, transport, and refine the crude oil commodity, with the intent that the U.K. should become self-sufficient in crude oil at the earliest possible

moment. Said consortium will be selected by the government of the U.S. All drilling equipment, ships, rigs, refineries, and all material, equipment, and supplies shall be purchased from and supplied by American companies and consultants;

AND PROVIDED FURTHER, that all workmen and consultants, or any other persons employed in said work, shall be U.S. nationals, it being the expressed intent that all U.K. trade unions and their membership be excluded from direct or indirect participation in the expeditious completion of the North Sea crude oil development; to this end, the U.K. will enact such legislation as it considers appropriate to give effect to this condition;

AND PROVIDED FURTHER, that the U.K. undertakes to employ its armed forces to protect any installations of the consortium, whether on or off shore, and similarly, to protect their consultants, workmen, or any other persons engaged by them.

7. The cost of the aforesaid work shall be paid for by the U.S. but shall be for the account of the U.K. It shall be repaid to the U.S. out of production on a per-barrel levy, to be calculated when the capital cost of the development of the North Sea crude oil to the level of self-sufficiency is accomplished.

8. Title to all the aforesaid works shall be vested in the government of the United Kingdom.

9. The U.S. will have first call (at world market prices) on all surplus crude oil and natural gas production from the North Sea fields.

IT IS UNDERSTOOD that this memorandum of agreement has been approved and accepted by the President of the United States under the powers vested in him by the Constitution of the United States of America and that the appropriate leaders of the Senate and the House of Representatives of the Congress have given their concurrence to the provisions of this document;

AND FURTHER, that the acceptance of this proposal by the government of the United Kingdom is to be open until but not after twelve noon on Thursday, the 8th day of July.

Daniel Sheppard,
President of the United
States of America.

Michael Hobson,
Chancellor of the Exchequer,
for the Government of the
United Kingdom.

The Prime Minister leaned slowly forward, placed the document on the table and slipped off his glasses, holding one end in his mouth as he contemplated the ramifications of the memorandum. Then he looked at the Secretary of State. "Well, Jessica, I guess we have no choice. Sorry – I really didn't mean to sound ungrateful. Your government, the people of the United States, have been exceedingly generous, far more than I had hoped for.

"It's just that our own ineptitude in handling the North Sea fields really shows what a pathetic position we're in. Personally and nationalistically, I find the concept of letting your own people take over the North Sea work totally unacceptable. The trade unions are going to go stark raving mad over this one." He stopped, reached down with his functioning hand to pick up his cigar, and had a puff. Then he sat back and went on.

"On the other hand, as I said, we have no choice. Yes, it's

time for a National Government. We can't fight over this in the House of Commons. We've got to meet it with a united front. Parliament has to tell the unions that this is what must be done. We have no alternative."

Cradling her brandy snifter and looking into it, Jessica asked, "Will you accept the memorandum?"

Sands' reply was quick and emphatic. "Yes, of course I will, Jessica. That document represents the only opportunity to turn Britain around and to get the nation going again, to get us on the road to energy self-sufficiency. Then we can bind up the wound on the side of our nation through which we've been pouring our life blood into the hands of the OPEC countries. The terms are tough, but the times for Britain and her people are even tougher. There must be dramatic, fast action. There must be results."

He tapped the memorandum as it lay on the table and leaned forward. "This gives us a new start, provided . . ." his voice trailed off.

"Provided what?" Jessica was looking him directly in the eye now.

"The other key matter." They both knew what it was. There was no mention of it in the document. Jessica had said not a word about it. If Britain was to be truly turned around – returned to the prosperous, productive, profit-making, energetic, dynamic nation it once was – one further ingredient would have to be added to those contained in the memorandum of agreement. Although the document's terms would provide a turn-around point, many months would be needed to implement it. Perhaps five years would pass before the U.K.'s extremely high unemployment would begin to decline, before food and energy shortages would diminish, and before the siege over Britain's economy would be lifted. It would not be lifted unless millions of people emigrated from the British Isles.

"What about it, Jessica? What about the open-gate immigration policy? Its acceptance by the United States is as critical as the generous money and oil provisions you've made."

This was the difficult question. Secretary Swift hesitated, collecting her line of reasoning. "As you can well appreciate, Jeremy, this has been a most difficult matter for the President and for us who advise him. He's had to consult with all the congressional leaders. I can tell you there's been strong, strong opposition by the American labour union leaders. We think we're well on our way out of the recession that began in 1975 – automobile sales are up, people are buying again, unemployment has gone down 2 per cent in the last two months. It's back down to 6 per cent, which means about five and a half million people out of work. As you know, it was up as high as 10 per cent in late 1975. The stock market is strong and the Petro-dollars have started to recycle in quantity back into our system. In spite of all the good signs, the labour leaders, particularly in the automotive and steel unions, have taken the position that unemployment is still far too high. If the United States was to accept say, two million people, that would mean another 700,000 job-seekers on the market."

The Prime Minister protested. "But a good percentage of those people are highly trained, skilled workers, professional people. They can make an enormous contribution to America."

"That's only partly true, Jeremy. About 60 per cent of your unemployed are in the unskilled class. There would be between 400,000 and 500,000 of them dumped on our market within a year."

Again the Prime Minister protested. "But surely, with your population – you're well over 220 million – surely you can accept two million people in a year. It's less than 1 per cent, a drop in the bucket. Spread them out across the country and you'll never know they're there."

Jessica Swift smiled at him.

"Beautiful, beautiful woman," he thought to himself.

"That's exactly the argument the President used on the Congressional leaders," she argued, "and for that matter, on the labour union bosses. He said he knew what all the numbers were and what the unemployment situation was, but he was talking about human beings, people who were deprived, people who were refugees from an economic disaster. He said that America was built on compassion, that America could not turn her back on the British."

Apprehensively, the Prime Minister put the question. "So what's the decision of your government?"

The Secretary of State stood up, the Prime Minister of the United Kingdom rising with her. Formally, but smiling, she announced, "I'm instructed by the President of the United States of America to inform you that the government of the United States accepts the open-gate immigration policy and will welcome all Britons who wish to come to our country within the next twelve months. And he has instructed me to offer to you all the assistance my department can put at your disposal and to aid in making arrangements for aircraft and ships to facilitate the movement."

Jeremy Sands was overjoyed. He moved quickly around the table, put his arm around Jessica Swift and kissed her gently on the mouth. "God bless you, Jessica."

She chastised him playfully. "You should have said 'God bless America.'"

11:17 PM
Office of the Prime Minister of Canada
Centre Block, Parliament Buildings
Ottawa, Canada

While Prime Minister Sands was meeting with Secretary Swift, his aide, Prentice, had been informed that the Canadian Cabinet was still in session; that when the British leader left his meeting with the American Secretary of State he should go directly to the Centre Block of the Parliament Buildings. They would be met at the main door by Roussel's principal secretary, Pierre Pratte.

When Sands and Prentice arrived at the brightly lit Parliament Buildings, their limousine had to proceed slowly as they moved past the East Block and up the grade toward the gothic arch of the main entrance to the Centre Block. Both the huge, grassed square in front of it and the roadway were filled with hundreds of people carrying banners and posters protesting against the possible mass influx of Britons. Apparently they were all French-Canadians. Shouting in French, they held signs such as, "*anglais*, stay at home," and "*Vive le Québec libre*," and "Quebec out if *anglais* in." Nowhere was there a banner to be seen in support of letting the British in. Not one.

As planned, Pratte was waiting for them at the main door. He greeted them peremptorily and said nothing as they made their way to the Prime Minister's office. With the assistance of the Royal Canadian Mounted Police and the commission-aires, he shepherded Sands and Prentice across the rotunda to the elevator, then along the third floor corridor to Roussel's office, 311 South. Sands expected Pratte to call down to the Cabinet Room to inform the Canadian Prime Minister that Sands was available to go into the meeting.

Instead, Pratte said as they entered Roussel's suite, "The Prime Minister is waiting for you in his office, sir." He pointed to the heavy wooden door leading to the corner office in front of them.

Sands stopped short in surprise. "I thought he was in Cabinet."

"No sir, the Cabinet meeting finished about ten minutes ago."

It was a shocked Jeremy Sands who confronted Prime Minister Roussel as soon as their perfunctory formalities were out of the way and they were alone. "Joseph, Pratte informs me the Cabinet meeting is over. Surely you're going to give me a chance to speak to Cabinet. You received my message, didn't you?"

Roussel shrugged. "Yes, I got your message, but there was nothing I could do. The Cabinet had been debating the question since eight o'clock. The money support – we can go for a two billion dollar loan, no more – and the food question were no problem. But on the immigration request there was a terrible fight. It was just awful. *Incroyable.* Please, Jeremy, sit down." He motioned toward the settee in front of the huge, stone, fireless fireplace. Sands sat, favouring his left arm as Roussel began to pace across the floor in front of his desk. Looking away from the British Prime Minister, waving and gesticulating as he spoke excitedly, Roussel injected a French word when it came easier than the English.

"Sure, I got your message. But like I say, there was nothing

254

I could do. The Cabinet wanted to get on with the debate and the decision.''

Sands pressed. ''But Prime Minister, you knew I was meeting with the Secretary of State at the airport. As a matter of courtesy, if nothing else, you could have instructed the Cabinet to wait!''

Roussel kept pacing, shaking his head in response to that remark. ''There was nothing I could do to hold them, *rien*, I assure you.''

Sands went on. ''I know the immigration question had divided the Cabinet and the country.''

''Divided!'' Roussel shouted. ''Divided! *Mon dieu*, this must be the worst crisis since Confederation. Keeping this country together is difficult at the best of times. The separatists in Quebec want to separate. British Columbia and the west are always mad at central Canada. The Maritimers are always grumbling. But today is the day. This hour will have been the hour. The Cabinet made its decision, Prime Minister, and I chose not to force them to wait for you. I can assure you there is nothing that you could have said which would have changed the mind of any one of them, so don't feel badly that you didn't have your chance. Perhaps for you it is better that you did not.''

Roussel was still pacing. The British Prime Minister got to his feet.

''What is the decision?''

Roussel stopped, looking directly at Sands. ''It was very difficult, the worst meeting I've ever been through. But I took the position before we started that I would go along with the decision of the Cabinet, whichever way it went, notwithstanding the fact that I'm French-Canadian, that I'm intensely loyal to Quebec, to my French-Canadian comrades, my culture, and my language. Nevertheless, I am a federalist. I believe this country is a great one with enormous potential. In any event, I said I would go along with what the majority of the Cabinet decided, regardless. Yes, Prime Minister, the Cabinet has made its decision and the split is deep and wide."

There was a knock on the door. The Canadian Prime Minister went to it, opened it, received an envelope, shut the door, tore open the envelope, read it quickly, and looked at Sands. "The split, it is a catastrophe. Since the Cabinet meeting finished, I have lost two ministers. This . . . " he waved the letter at Sands, "is the third resignation. I'm sure there are more to come."

He commenced pacing again. "And secession, there will be secession, absolutely no doubt about it in my mind. I will fight it, but not with guns, not with military arms, but only with words, only with words." He stopped his movement, again looking at the British Prime Minister. "Isn't it strange? We've been worrying about national unity in Canada ever since I can remember. And what happens to destroy Confederation? It is an event in the United Kingdom, not an event in Canada." He shook his head in disbelief.

Looking squarely into the eyes of the Prime Minister of the United Kingdom, the Prime Minister of Canada, Joseph Roussel, spoke slowly. "Prime Minister, the decision of the Cabinet, the decision of the government of Canada, on the question of whether Canada will accept a mass immigration of people from the United Kingdom, on, as you put it, an open-gate basis is. . . ."